THE CURIOUS CORONATION

Eight invitations mysteriously sent to Louise and Jean Dana for the same teen-age pageant start these young detectives on a harrowing series of incidents. They must locate the fabulous stolen jeweled crown to be worn by the winning contestant. Their first clue leads to a hunt for the statue of a mythical bird. They find this prize only to lose it, but do not give up. One of the contestants is kidnapped. After receiving a strange message, Louise and Jean, with their friends Ken and Chris, embark on a dangerous rescue. Readers will hurry through this book to see if Louise and Jean succeed.

The rescuers urged the man to swim toward them.

The *Dana Girls* Mystery Stories

THE CURIOUS CORONATION

By Carolyn Keene

GROSSET & DUNLAP

Publishers   *New York*

CONTENTS

THE
CURIOUS
CORONATION

CHAPTER I

Strange Invitations

"THERE is a big batch of mail for you girls today," the postman said. He smiled at the Danas. "Maybe one letter has a mystery for you to solve," he teased, handing the bundle to them.

"I hope so," they replied, grinning.

The pleasant man had known Louise and Jean Dana since they were little. Louise, now seventeen and a year older than her sister, was dark-haired while Jean was blond.

The girls hurried into the living room and sat down to untie the package of letters.

"Great!" Louise cried. "Here's a letter from Ken." He was her favorite date.

Jean's eyes sparkled. "And there's one for me from Chris." Then she exclaimed, "Eight envelopes exactly alike, except for the handwriting! One, two, three, four are addressed to you. The rest are for me!"

"They look like invitations," Louise said, and

Mrs. Marcia Menken,
chairman,
and members of the committee
for the
Student Culture and Talent
Pageant
cordially invite you to attend
the coronation of
their empress
on August twentieth at
eight in the evening in
Memorial Hall
(next to the armory)
Newport Beach
R.S.V.P. by August tenth

"Eight just alike!" Jean exclaimed. "Four to you, Louise. Four to me!"

she started to open one, which was slightly heavier than the others. "Yes, it is an invitation, and here's a letter inside."

"What does it say?" Jean asked.

Louise read the message hurriedly, then said, "How amazing! I'm invited to be a judge at a pageant at Newport Beach."

"What kind?" her sister inquired.

"A student culture-and-talent pageant for teen-age girls. It's being held in Newport Beach."

Jean thought for a moment, then said, "That must be the same event our boarding school was asked to participate in. Remember, Mrs. Crandall said she wouldn't permit any of the students at Starhurst to sign up."

Both girls laughed, then Jean opened the fattest of her envelopes. It was a duplicate of the one Louise had received. "I'm to be a judge too." She giggled. "Even if we couldn't try out for the contest, the headmistress can't keep us from being judges now that school is out for the summer!"

"It sounds like fun," Louise remarked.

At this moment their aunt, Harriet Dana, walked into the room to claim her letters and magazines from the pile the postman had left. Louise and Jean had lived in Oak Falls with Aunt Harriet and her brother, Ned Dana, since the girls became orphans many years before.

Miss Dana was motherly, kind, and gentle, yet

strict when the occasion demanded it. Uncle Ned, the captain of an ocean liner was rarely at home. At this moment he was in Europe.

Louise removed her aunt's mail from the stack and handed it to her. Then she said, "Jean and I have a little mystery here." She told Aunt Harriet about the envelopes, saying that the two with letters were addressed in one handwriting, while the other six were written in similar, but somewhat different styles. "We were just going to examine them."

Their curiosity piqued, the Dana girls opened the rest of the envelopes one by one while Aunt Harriet watched eagerly. All were engraved invitations to attend the student culture-and-talent pageant. None, however, contained a note.

Aunt Harriet asked, "Why would anyone send you so many invitations?"

The girls shrugged and Jean suggested that perhaps several members on the committee had addressed the envelopes. By some mistake, Louise's and Jean's names could have been on four lists.

"Something tells me that isn't the answer," Louise said. "I think I'll phone the chairman, Mrs. Menken, and ask her. By the way, Aunt Harriet, is it all right for Jean and me to be judges?"

"I think it is quite an honor," Miss Dana replied. "Yes, go ahead and accept."

As Louise was about to call Mrs. Menken in

Newport Beach, the phone rang. She answered it. A weak voice at the other end of the line was saying, "Louise, is that you?"

"Yes. Who is this?"

Barely audible, the caller answered, "This is Evelyn—Evelyn Starr. I'm calling from Newport Beach. Louise, I've been in a horrible automobile accident. I'm in the hospital. My brother is in Europe. Please, can you and Jean come to see me right away?"

Louise was stunned. Evelyn Starr, their closest friend, attended the Starhurst School for Girls with them. They knew she had gone to Newport Beach for a vacation.

"Of course we'll come," Louise replied. "Where are you?"

"At the Newport Beach Hospital. But please hurry! I'm in bad shape."

"We'll be there as soon as we can make it," Louise promised. "Evie, keep your chin up!"

Aunt Harriet and Jean were distressed by the news. Miss Dana said, "You two take my new car and go immediately."

In one breath both girls said, "Please come with us, Aunt Harriet."

Miss Dana smiled. "All right. Perhaps I can be of some help to Evelyn. This is dreadful."

Louise called the Starfish Motel in Newport Beach to make reservations. Then she joined her relatives in the kitchen. They were speaking to the young woman who helped them with the house-work. Cora Apple, nicknamed Applecore by Jean, was told that the Danas were going to pack im-mediately and leave.

Cora's eyes became very large. "Why? You didn't say anything about it before."

Louise explained. All the while Cora kept mum-bling, "Poor Evelyn!" She liked this friend of the Danas very much. "Oh, why am I so nervous? Don't let anything happen to you on the road. And give Miss Evelyn my best wishes. And do you think she'd like some of my homemade cookies?"

With that, she opened the oven door and pulled out a large sheet of the delicious-smelling little cakes. Flustered, she had forgotten to use a pot-holder and now could not hold the pan. It clattered to the floor and many of the cookies broke.

"Oh dear, oh dear!" Cora wailed. "I'm just no good at all!" She began to cry.

"Don't cry, Cora," Aunt Harriet said. "We all have little mishaps. You pick up the cookies that aren't damaged and brush off the crumbs. We'll take them along. And now, Louise, Jean, and I are going upstairs to pack."

On the way the sisters stopped to examine the other mail they had received. They decided to take it all with them and to look at the extra invitations more carefully in the car.

"I have a hunch," Louise said, "that there really is something behind this. I want to study each invitation."

A short time later the Danas were ready to go. Fortunately their wardrobes were adequate for the trip, including the festive weekend contest and pageant.

"But at this moment I don't feel very festive," Jean confessed. "I'm terribly worried about Evelyn."

"I am too," Louise admitted.

About halfway to Newport Beach they stopped for gas. While an attendant was filling the tank, Jean opened her tote bag so she might read one of the invitations, then began to rummage frantically in her bag.

"What's the matter?" Miss Dana asked. "Did you lose something?"

Jean said she could find only three of her four invitations. "Louise, do you have an extra one?"

Louise looked in her own tote bag. She had only those addressed to her.

"Oh dear!" said Jean. She started to get out of the car. "I'm going to call home and ask Applecore to find the fourth invitation and send it to me."

Jean went to a phone booth and made the call. The others watched her face fall. Finally she came out of the booth and stepped back into the car.

"Cora found the invitation. She said it was near the wastebasket, and she thought I had meant to throw it away. She has already burned it along with other trash."

"That's a shame," Aunt Harriet said. "But maybe you won't need it. I take it you girls think there might be something mysterious about those extra invitations." The sisters nodded.

The rest of the way to Newport Beach there was little conversation. The Danas went directly to the hospital and asked where Evelyn Starr's room was.

"She's not supposed to have visitors," the receptionist said after looking up Evelyn's card.

Louise quickly explained that Evelyn had asked them to come. "We're her closest friends," she said, "and she has no relatives nearby."

The woman smiled and replied, "I'll find out from the floor nurse." In a few minutes she told them, "It's all right for you three to go up."

The Danas' hearts were pounding as they walked down the eighth-floor corridor to the injured girl's room. She and her roommate were dozing, but Evelyn immediately opened her eyes when the Danas walked in.

She smiled faintly and whispered, "You darlings! You came! Now I know I'm going to get better."

The visitors had already decided not to make her talk, but she volunteered information about the accident. "I was riding between two boys in the front seat of a car. There was a couple in the back seat. Suddenly the driver seemed to lose control. The car swerved and he smashed into a tree. The two in the back seat weren't hurt, but the three of us in the front ended up in the hospital."

At this moment a nurse came in and told the Danas that the ten minutes allowed for visiting were up. The three rose and said good-by to Evelyn.

"We'll be back tomorrow," Louise promised. "In the meantime, here are some homemade cookies Applecore sent you. If you want us, call the Starfish Motel in Newport Beach. Bye, honey."

Out in the hall, Jean asked the nurse how seriously Evelyn had been injured.

"She has a broken leg," the nurse replied. "And lots of bruises. She was in a state of shock when she was brought in here. Poor Evelyn has been so lonesome. I'm glad you came."

"Phone if you need us," Louise suggested and told her where they were staying. The nurse promised to do so.

The Starfish Motel was very attractive. Cars entered through an arch and followed a circular driveway up to the main door. At the center of the large grass plot in front of the entrance was a huge starfish made of flowers. The three-story, rambling building was situated on a bluff above the ocean. Below was a sandy beach, which could be reached by steps.

"What a great place!" Louise said admiringly.

Aunt Harriet nodded. "Don't let solving the

mystery spoil your good time here. Enjoy this place and all it has to offer as much as you possibly can."

As soon as the two girls were settled in their room, with Aunt Harriet in the one adjoining theirs, Jean said, "Louise, curiosity is overcoming me. I'm going to call Mrs. Menken, the chairman of the contest, tell her we'll be glad to be judges, and ask about all the invitations we received. Maybe she'll have an explanation."

Jean dialed the number and introduced herself, then explained why she and her sister had come to Newport Beach so far ahead of the pageant.

"I'm sorry your friend had an accident," the woman said. "And my apologies for your receiving the invitations so late. Sometimes I get so busy I forget things I'm supposed to do."

Jean told the chairman about the six extra invitations that had arrived in the mail.

"Can you tell us why?"

"That's strange," the woman replied in a worried tone of voice. "One person addressed all of the invitations we sent out. Do you think something is wrong?" she asked in alarm.

CHAPTER II

A Threat

"WE don't know whether something is wrong or not," Louise told Mrs. Menken. "But receiving six extra invitations in different handwritings seems kind of strange to us."

The chairman of the pageant laughed lightly. "I don't know how anyone else got hold of the list, but I have an idea that a person, or persons, was playing a joke on you. Right now, what interests me more is, are you going to accept the invitation to be teen-age judges?"

"Yes, we are," Louise replied. "We were going to write you a formal acceptance."

"Oh, don't bother to do that," the woman said. "I'm so happy that you will be able to help the older judges decide who the winner and the four runners-up will be."

The next morning Louise woke early. She put on her robe and slippers, then pulled out the other invitations from her tote bag. She opened one and read it thoroughly. Suddenly she realized that one C had a barely visible circle around it.

"I believe this is part of a message," she thought, "circled in pencil."

At once the young detective began going over the whole invitation carefully. In a few moments she spotted a W that was also lightly circled.

By this time Jean had awakened and asked her sister what she was doing. When Louise told her, Jean hopped out of bed and looked over Louise's shoulder.

"Oh, I see the letter S!" she exclaimed. "But what in the world could C, W, and S stand for?"

Louise said she had no idea and wondered if it even pertained to the pageant.

"You mean it may be a signal to us as judges?" Jean asked. "Could they be initials of contestants?"

"At this point I suppose we could guess anything," her sister replied. "Right now I think we should dress and have breakfast. I want to get to the hospital as soon as we can."

Just as they finished dressing, Aunt Harriet opened the door between the two rooms and walked in. Saying good morning, she kissed both her nieces and asked if they had slept well.

"Oh yes," Louise answered. "And we started working on the puzzle of the extra invitations." She showed her aunt the letters they had found with the lightly penciled rings around them.

Aunt Harriet was amazed and could offer no explanation. "I guess you'll just have to find more letters in order to solve this mystery."

As soon as visiting hours started at the hospital, Louise and Jean set off to see Evelyn. Aunt Harriet had said she would not go this time. Once more the girls took the elevator to the eighth floor. As they walked toward Evelyn's room, they could hear excited conversation between interns and nurses. Louise and Jean were anxious. Had something happened to Evelyn?

The two girls became more and more frightened as they approached. Just then a stretcher bed was wheeled from the room. A blanket had been pulled up to the patient's mouth and a towel was wound around the head so that only the nose and closed eyes showed.

"Please step aside!" one of the interns ordered the visitors. "Perhaps you'd better go to the solarium and wait."

"Is—is the patient Evelyn Starr?"

A nurse replied, "No. She's still in her room. If you want to see her, wait here a few minutes."

The nurse and the interns went off with the patient while two aides stepped into the room.

Louise and Jean sagged against the wall. Although they were over their fright, they felt weak. In a few minutes the aides came out and said that it was all right for them to go in and see Evelyn.

"But please don't stay very long," one requested.

Louise and Jean entered. Evelyn appeared so much better than she had the day before that they were thrilled. She smiled at them and said, "You two look like ghosts! What happened to you?"

"We thought you were being wheeled out," Louise explained. "Thank goodness you're not only here, but you're so much better!"

Evelyn smiled. "Your visit yesterday was like a tonic. The doctors and nurses are amazed that I've made such wonderful progress."

She asked the Danas to tell her what else they had been doing, so they brought her up-to-date on the invitations.

"How interesting!" Evelyn said.

Then she mentioned that she had some news of her own. A cablegram had come that morning from her brother. He had left Europe and was on his way to China. He would be there for a short while on secret government work and could not give her an address.

Evelyn added wistfully, "I'm sure if he knew about my accident, he'd come right home. Oh, how I'd love to see him!"

Louise endeavored to cheer her up by saying, "Probably by the time he arrives, you'll be entirely well. And I'm sure he'd rather see you that way. Don't you think so?"

Evelyn smiled. "You always have the right

answer, Louise Dana. Of course that would be better! I wanted to tell you a little more about my accident. I'm really lucky to be alive. The boy who was driving was going at a reckless speed. He went around the corner very fast, and couldn't make it. That was when we skidded and smashed into the tree."

"His name is Moss Engels. The boy on the other side of me was Eric Reese."

"Are they staying here?" Jean asked.

Evelyn shook her head. "They were taken to a hospital in another town. I think it's where they live. I met them at a dance here and we went driving afterward."

"Who were the couple in the rear seat?" Louise asked.

"I don't know. They didn't mention their names —just asked Moss if he'd drop them off at their home. He never had a chance to do it."

Louise glanced at her watch. The few minutes they were allowed to visit had long since passed. She said, "Jean, we'd better leave before the nurse shoos us out and won't let us visit again." She turned to Evelyn. "We'll be back to see you soon. Keep up the good work!"

As soon as they reached the motel, Louise and Jean began to inspect their puzzling invitations. Aunt Harriet came in and they gave her one of the letters. Presently she said, "Here's a ringed O. Will that help you?"

The girls went over the letters they had taken out so far. To them they added R, another W, another O, a T, an E, and an L. Finally they had two words that made sense, "Stole crow."

"I wish I knew what that other W stands for," Jean said.

"I think we should call Mrs. Menken," Louise suggested, "and tell her about this. She might have an idea."

When Louise made the call, Mrs. Menken could offer no help with the puzzle, but she graciously invited the girls to stop at her home that afternoon.

"I have something unusual to show you," she said.

When they reached her lovely house, the girls noticed that it was furnished with fine pieces of Asiatic furniture and draperies.

Mrs. Menken smiled. "You see, I love Asiatic antiques, so I decided to have an Asiatic theme for the pageant. Come, I will show you my prize," she said. "By the way, you must promise not to tell anyone about this. I will use it on the final night."

She led them into a rear room, where there was a locked cabinet. She took the key from inside a vase standing nearby, and opened the ornate door. On a pedestal inside was an exquisite crown.

"It's beautiful!" Louise said, and Jean added, "And very unusual. Have you any idea who wore it?"

"Oh yes," Mrs. Menken replied, "an ancient

empress in China. I forget her name at the moment. I purchased the crown recently when I was abroad." She chuckled. "I paid a tremendous price for it. Perhaps I was foolish. But I absolutely fell in love with the crown."

At this moment the front doorbell rang. Quickly Mrs. Menken closed the cabinet and locked it. She put the key back into the empty vase, then went to the front door.

A moment later she brought in a very attractive girl, whom she introduced as Sally Benson.

"Sally is a nineteen year old student from the University of Louisiana," she said, "and has entered our contest as a singer."

Louise and Jean thought they had never seen a more beautiful girl. She was blond, with big blue, sparkling eyes. Her features were perfect and she had a gracious, friendly manner. But a few seconds later her expression changed to one of worry, and she admitted she was very upset.

"I've been threatened!" she explained. "A man telephoned me at the motel and said if I didn't get out of the pageant I would be harmed so I couldn't appear in it."

"How dreadful!" Louise said.

"I don't blame you for being worried," Jean added.

Mrs. Menken did not seem the least bit troubled. She put an arm around Sally and said, "I'm sure there's nothing to this. Someone is trying to play a joke on you."

Louise and Jean disagreed but said nothing. The woman's remark made Sally feel better, so the Danas decided to change the subject.

"Sally," said Louise, "would you sing something for us?"

The girl smiled. "All right."

The three sat down while Sally stood near the grand piano, but sang without accompaniment. When she finished two winsome Chinese lullabies, the other three applauded enthusiastically.

"They're lovely, Sally," Mrs. Menken said.

The Danas nodded and each thought, "What a gorgeous voice!" Aloud they thanked her.

Jean and Louise announced they must leave, and asked if Sally had driven herself.

"No, I came in a cab," the girl replied.

"Then we'll take you back," Louise offered. "Where are you staying?"

"At the Starfish Motel, with the other girls."

"So are we," Jean told her.

"Oh good," Sally said. "Will you be here for the pageant?"

Mrs. Menken told her that Louise and Jean were to be teen-age judges. Sally smiled. "That's great. But I wouldn't want your job for a million dollars!"

Everyone laughed. Then the girls said good-by

to Mrs. Menken. Louise drove directly toward the motel. There was a large parking lot in the rear, and the Danas had already been assigned a space. As they entered the area through an archway, Louise jammed on her brakes. Two men, one on each side, leaped toward the car and peered into it.

One of the men stared at their passenger, then ordered, "Sally Benson, come out of there!"

CHAPTER III

True or False?

"No!" Sally screamed, as the two men tried to open the locked car doors.

Louise did not wait. She gunned the motor and the car shot ahead. The two men had jumped aside. Jean and Sally got good glimpses of their faces.

Within seconds, Louise reached the motel entrance. Sally unlocked the door on her side, jumped out, and raced up the steps.

In the meantime, an attendant spoke to the Dana girls. Louise told him what had happened and asked if he would take the car.

"I think we should call the police," he said, startled.

"I do too," Louise replied.

The man picked up a nearby phone and asked the office to call the police. Then he requested that a second attendant be sent outside to go on a search with him.

Louise thanked the man, and the two Danas hopped out of the car. They went directly into the lobby. Sally, shaking with fright, had waited for them to come in.

"Please walk to my room with me," she requested.

As soon as they reached it, Sally flung herself on one of the beds and began to cry softly. "I'll never forget that awful face on my side!" she said. "It didn't seem human. Did you see him, Jean?"

"Yes. And I agree it was horrible. Personally I think the man is Asiatic, but he must have worn some kind of make-up putty to disguise his features."

Louise was interested. "I can't understand how he knows you, Sally. You didn't recognize him, but he called you by name."

Sally sat up. "I never saw that awful creature in my life, and I didn't recognize the other man in the plaid coat. He wasn't so ugly."

"No," said Jean. "He'd be easy to spot."

Just then the door to the room opened and another pretty teen-ager walked in.

"Girls," Sally said, "this is my roommate, Judy Irish. This is Louise Dana and her sister Jean."

Judy was very friendly, and the Danas liked her at once. Sally told her what had happened at the entrance to the parking lot.

Judy was incensed. "Did you find out why they wanted you?" she asked.

"They ordered me out of the car. That's all I know."

"How ghastly!" Judy said. "Do you think they wanted to kidnap you?"

The Dana girls had thought of that, but Sally had not. She was horrified at the idea. In a shaky voice she asked, "Why would anyone want to kidnap me?"

Louise put an arm around her. "Whether they did or didn't, I wouldn't worry about it. But don't leave the motel unless you're with a group."

Judy nodded. "That's sensible. I'll try to look after Sally."

Louise and Jean said good-by. They immediately went to Aunt Harriet's room. Their lovely relative was seated at the desk.

"Hi, girls!" she greeted them. "I thought I'd write your Uncle Ned and mention the mysterious invitations you received. Have you been up to any more mischief for me to tell him about?"

Louise and Jean sat down and told their aunt about the afternoon's adventures. Miss Dana thought the empress's crown sounded intriguing, but she was more concerned about the man who had ordered Sally out of the car.

Louise said, "I can't help but think it has something to do with the pageant. Jean, let's see if we can figure out any more from the invitations. We might find additional lightly ringed letters to put into some kind of message."

The girls went to their room. As Louise worked, she kept looking at the sheet of paper on which she had written the words "stole crow." Suddenly she said, "Jean, do you suppose the phrase could be 'stolen crown'?"

Jean said that if they could find two ringed N's, Louise was probably right. In a few minutes the girls found them.

Jean said, "It could be either 'stolen crown' or 'crown stolen.' Louise, do you think it could have anything to do with the crown Mrs. Menken has?"

"That's a wonderful deduction," Louise admitted.

Just then the telephone rang. Jean answered it. A man's voice asked, "Are you one of the Danas?"

"Yes," Jean replied.

"Is your car license number EVX-71-825?"

Jean did not know whether to answer or not. Instead she said, "Who is this?"

There was no reply. The caller had hung up.

Aunt Harriet walked into the room and asked, "Who was that?"

Jean explained. Her aunt did not wait a second. She picked up the phone and reported the incident to the office. The man on duty said he would send people outside to guard the Danas' car.

"Thank you," Aunt Harriet said. "If you find out anything, please let us know."

He promised to do so and later reported that

there had been no sign of any suspicious characters. Two, rather than one guard, would be kept out there at all times.

"That's a big relief to us," Aunt Harriet said.

After dinner Louise and Jean introduced their aunt to Sally, Judy, and several other contestants they had met. Miss Dana smiled and said, "Every one of you should wear a crown!"

The girls laughed and Judy said that was true. "It would be good entertainment for the audience, anyway."

The Danas talked with the group for a few minutes. Sally then suggested that they all go downstairs to the private lounge that had been rented for rehearsals by the contestants.

"I want you to meet everyone," she said to Louise, Jean, and Aunt Harriet.

They all went to the first floor. At the end of the lounge were a piano, a record player, and enough space for the entrants to practice marching.

Sally explained that so far no rehearsals had been announced for that night. The girls had gathered just to have fun. One tall, slender young woman dressed in a black leotard and white tights was practicing cartwheels across the narrow stage. Behind her stood a trim girl in cut-off blue jeans. As the young acrobat tumbled into a final somersault, a spectator rolled her eyes dramatically.

"You're making me dizzy!" she exclaimed, shaking her head. A funny expression on her face brought loud guffaws from the girls. While they were talking and laughing, the door opened and Mrs. Menken came in. At once the contestants began to clap. She acknowledged their warm greeting with a wave of her hand.

Aunt Harriet whispered to Louise and Jean, "She probably has private matters to talk over with these girls. We'd better go."

Before leaving, the three spoke to Mrs. Menken, and Jean added, "We have something important to discuss with you. May we see you when this meeting is finished?"

"You mean something to do with the mystery?" the chairman asked.

Jean said yes, but it could wait.

"Suppose I come to your room after I leave here?" Mrs. Menken suggested.

The Danas agreed to this. They sauntered into the lobby and watched a television show but kept an eye on the door through which she would come.

Half an hour later Mrs. Menken reappeared. The Danas walked over to her and they all went to Louise and Jean's room.

As soon as they were seated, Mrs. Menken said, "Now tell me what's on your mind. I can hardly wait to hear it."

The girls briefly brought her up-to-date on the mysterious invitations, saying they had figured out two words from the marked letters. They were either "stolen crown" or "crown stolen."

"By any chance, do you think it could refer to the empress's crown you have in your cabinet?" Louise asked.

Mrs. Menken turned pale. "Stolen!" she exclaimed. "Oh, if that's true, I want nothing to do with it. I paid a very high price for that piece, but I won't keep the empress's crown if it's stolen property!"

Aunt Harriet spoke in a calm voice. "Maybe your crown wasn't stolen. It's possible the invitations refer to some other crown."

Louise asked Mrs. Menken where she had purchased the unusual headpiece.

"In Hong Kong. I saw it in a glass case. A man who was coming to New York offered to bring it to America, since I was going on an extensive tour and didn't want to carry it with me. I was afraid I might lose it. The man was highly recommended by the shop owner and the hotel manager, and he did carry out his promise. He mailed the crown to me from New York."

The Danas glanced at one another. They felt the woman had been very foolish.

Louise asked Mrs. Menken if she was sure she could definitely identify it as the one she had purchased. The woman thought for a few moments, then said, "Yes, I sort of remember one thing. Do you recall the long strings of jade beads at the sides to cover the wearer's ears?"

Jean and Louise nodded.

"Whoever created the crown," Mrs. Menken continued, "made one side a little shorter than the other."

"Oh, that's a wonderful clue!" Jean exclaimed. She was eager to see it and asked Mrs. Menken if she were ready to leave.

The woman nodded. "But I didn't drive. I came here by cab. Do you girls have a car?"

"Yes," Louise replied.

"Then suppose you drive me home and we'll take a close look at the empress's crown in my cabinet."

She and the three Danas went to the girls' car and set off. They made sure that all the windows were closed and the doors locked. Louise and Jean had not forgotten the strange anonymous phone call they had received and were still worried.

As soon as they reached Mrs. Menken's home, she and the Danas hurried inside. She went ahead to turn on the light in the room in which the cabinet stood.

"Now we'll find out what the truth is," she said.

Within seconds she had opened the door and turned on an electric bulb in the top of the cabinet. The girls could see at once that all the danglers of jade stones on both sides were exactly the same length!

Now they concentrated on the gems themselves. Although Louise and Jean were not experts on jade, they thought these looked dull and lifeless. Probably they had not cost much. Jean ventured to tell this to the owner.

Suddenly Mrs. Menken cried out, "These are of very inferior quality. I've been robbed! And of a large sum of money. This crown is a clever substitute but it is not the gorgeous, authentic one I bought!"

CHAPTER IV

Unjust Accusation!

Louise and Jean were not surprised to hear that the crown in Mrs. Menken's cabinet was a substitute for the one she had purchased. They wondered, however, where the exchange had been made—in Hong Kong, on shipboard, or in New York.

She admitted that she was out of the house a great deal and there were many times when a burglar might have entered and stolen the original ancient crown.

"I blame myself!" she said, her eyes filling with tears. "I have been too trusting. Oh what shall I do?"

While Aunt Harriet was trying to soothe the indignant woman, the girls were whispering about what their next move should be. First, they must find out the name of the man who had brought the package to New York.

Louise asked Mrs. Menken. She thought a few moments, then said, "I can't remember his name, but I'll look for it and let you know. Oh, this memory of mine plays tricks on me all the time."

The Danas returned to their motel. Aunt Harriet went to bed directly, but Louise and Jean were too excited to sleep. They decided to work a little more on the rest of what seemed to be a hidden message in the invitations.

After concentrating on the letters for nearly an hour, the two girls found a circled G and an X.

"None of these makes any sense by itself," Jean commented. "Probably the missing letters were in the invitation burned by Applecore."

Louise added, "These letters don't belong to 'stolen crown.' I'm getting tired. Maybe in the morning we'll be more alert and can learn something else."

The sisters were yawning so much that they both giggled. They could hardly say good night to each other.

In the morning Mrs. Menken phoned them. "I have the name of the man who offered to bring the crown from Hong Kong," she said. "It was Charlie Ching."

Louise, who had taken the message, asked, "Is that his right name?"

Mrs. Menken said she really did not know and could not recall the sender's address on the package. "I don't see how we can find him."

"Surely he must have a passport," Louise told her. "We'll try to track that down."

She discussed the matter with Aunt Harriet and Jean. Miss Dana offered to help. She went into her own room and started making phone calls.

In the meantime, Louise and Jean worked on the invitations. But they were so interested in what Aunt Harriet might learn that they could not concentrate. The result was that they did not find any more clues. Finally Miss Dana came back into their room. She was smiling.

"You found out something?" Jean asked eagerly.

Their aunt replied that she had been very fortunate in locating a friend of Uncle Ned's who worked at the Passport Office in Washington. "He was most helpful. After I revealed that we are trying to track down a thief, he gave me the information we need. There are several Charles Chings with passports.

"But this is the big surprise," Aunt Harriet said. "One of them lives right here in Newport Beach!"

"Oh, that's wonderful!" Jean cried, and both girls hugged their aunt. Louise added, "You're a super detective yourself!"

Aunt Harriet laughed and asked the girls what they would do with her discovery.

Louise had already pulled out the phone book and was looking for Mr. Ching's number. She found it and exclaimed, "Here's a Dr. Charles Ching. It doesn't say what kind of a doctor he is."

Jean suggested that maybe the police could help

them. She called headquarters and learned that Dr. Ching was a professor.

"Why don't we go to see him before lunch?" Jean proposed.

The others agreed, and Louise wrote down the address. Dr. Ching's home, which was some distance out of town, was a large house with spacious grounds.

Louise parked and the three went to the front door. It was opened by a fine-looking, elderly Chinese man who smiled at the callers.

Aunt Harriet spoke for all the Danas. "Dr. Ching?"

"Yes."

"May we ask you a few questions? My nieces and I have come across a mystery that has to do with China. Perhaps you can help us solve it."

The professor invited them into his study and said he would be glad to do what he could. His wife was there and he introduced her. Both spoke perfect English and were most polite and gracious.

Louise said she realized that Professor Ching was not the Charles Ching for whom they were searching. "Do you know of any other man by that name?" she asked.

Dr. Ching shook his head and smiled. "No doubt there are many of them, but I do not happen to know any."

Jean asked the couple if they had been in Asia recently.

Mrs. Ching replied, "We haven't been over there

in years. Everything has changed so that we find it more comfortable to stay at home here. So many pleasant people teach at the university in town, and there are more parties than we can attend. It is a most enjoyable place, and we do not travel much any more."

Louise had been studying a strange picture on the wall. It seemed very old and somewhat resembled a map. She asked the professor what it meant.

"Ancient Chinese mythology is fascinating," he told his callers. "There are many, many stories of how the earth was formed. Most of them are based on the myth that our planet and the sun and the moon came from parts of the body of a great God. This picture represents the division.

"If you look closely, you will see that the earth is square and has an ocean on each side. The oceans connect and the ancients believed that if you went to the end of any one of the four sides, you would tumble off into the ocean. If you were lucky enough not to drown, a kind deity might pick you up and take you to the moon."

The Danas smiled and Louise remarked, "That story is quite different from the way our astronauts reached the moon."

"True," the professor said, smiling. "I hope you will come to see us again some time and I will tell you more stories. It is most ungracious of me, but it is necessary for me to leave. I have a class at the university."

The Danas stood up and thanked the Chings for their information. Louise said, "In solving a mystery, one must often follow and eliminate false clues."

"How true!" Mrs. Ching said. "I see you, too, are a philosopher. That's what my husband teaches. In life, don't we come upon many false clues to happiness or the truth before we find the real thing?"

Louise and Jean agreed. As the Danas were saying good-by to the Chings, Louise asked, "If you hear of another Charles Ching, will you please let us know? We'll be staying at the Starfish Motel for a while, at least until the student culture-and-talent pageant is over."

Jean added, "My sister and I are to be teen-age judges."

Mrs. Ching congratulated them and said that she and her husband planned to attend the affair. "We will be most eager to learn the results."

When the Danas reached the motel, Louise and Jean left their aunt and said they would go on to the hospital to see Evelyn.

"I'm sure she'll be expecting us," Jean remarked.

As the two sisters walked into her room a little while later, they found Evelyn sitting up in a chair. It occurred to Louise and Jean that the improvement in her condition should make their classmate happy. But instead Evelyn was very worried.

"What's the matter, honey?" Louise asked her.

For an answer, Evelyn handed her a letter. It was from a local lawyer and was neither friendly nor gracious. It stated that since Evelyn was responsible for the automobile accident, she would be required to pay for the damage to the car, as well as all medical bills for injuries to the driver.

"How can they blame you?" Jean asked. "You weren't driving the car!"

"Of course not. But read the rest!"

The letter went on to say that when the driver swerved to avoid a dog in the road, Evelyn had grabbed the wheel, causing the car to skid sideways and hit a tree.

"That's not true!" Evelyn cried out. "But I guess it's the driver's word against mine. I have no insurance for such a thing and, as you know, I have very little money." Evelyn began to cry, and said, "I can't face that lawyer. I'm too weak!"

She was becoming more hysterical by the moment. Louise and Jean tried their best to soothe her, even suggesting that they take over her case. But nothing consoled Evelyn.

A nurse, hearing the commotion, ran in. Without asking any questions, she immediately accused the Danas of upsetting the patient.

"Help me get her to bed!" the nurse ordered.

She and Louise lifted Evelyn into bed and covered her. Then the nurse turned to the Danas. "Leave at once!" she said.

She literally pushed them out the door and closed it!

CHAPTER V

Secretive Lawyer

On the way to their car both Louise and Jean admitted they were disturbed by the letter the lawyer had written to Evelyn, making preposterous demands.

"I suppose Evelyn's right—it's her word against the driver's," Louise remarked.

Jean added, "I thought in any car accident, the driver was always responsible."

Louise said that surely the lawyer would know this. "There must be some other reason why Evelyn could be accused."

Before driving off, the two girls read the letter again. It was from Aaron Brink, whose office was in downtown Newport Beach.

"Let's go to see him right away!" Jean urged.

The girls drove off. They went to the center of the Newport Beach shopping district and shortly arrived at the door of Mr. Brink's second-floor law office.

The girls walked in and introduced themselves to his secretary. According to a nameplate on her desk, she was Miss Dow.

"We'd like to talk to Mr. Brink," Louise said.

"I'm sorry but he's very busy," the woman replied. "Come back some other time."

Jean's eyes had been roving over the desk. They lighted on the appointment calendar for the day. It was blank!

Miss Dow noticed this and quickly covered the pad with her arm. In icy tones she repeated, "Mr. Brink is busy. Call again later."

The girls might have had no choice, but at that moment the inner door opened and a man walked out.

Seeing the two attractive girls, he walked over to them. "Can I be of help to you?" he asked, smiling flirtatiously.

The sisters ignored this, and Louise said they had a problem they would like very much to discuss with him.

"Step into my office," he invited them.

As the Danas disappeared inside, Miss Dow gave them a cold stare.

When the girls were seated, Jean announced that she and Louise were close friends of Evelyn Starr's. "She's very ill and upset over the letter you sent her."

Mr. Brink's friendly manner changed instantly. His eyes now narrowed, and his lips became a grim line.

Louise continued, "Apparently the person you spoke with has *mis*informed you. What Evelyn is being accused of is absolutely untrue!"

The lawyer shifted in his chair, then asked, "Were you girls with her at the time of the accident?"

"No," Louise said.

"Then your word is no good!" he shouted. "For your information, I have statements from everyone involved in the accident except Miss Starr." He rose. "Good day, and don't bother me again!"

The girls did not rise. They had more to say.

"I said good day," he repeated. "There's nothing more to discuss."

He pushed a buzzer on his desk and his secretary appeared.

"Please show these young ladies out," Mr. Brink said.

"That won't be necessary," Louise told him, her eyes flashing. "But this is not the last you have heard from us!"

Jean followed Louise, but on a hunch did not close the door tightly. The sisters had not proceeded far up the hall before she whispered, "I'm sure Aaron Brink will talk to Miss Dow. Let's listen for a clue!"

Louise nodded and the two tiptoed back to the lawyer's office. They were just in time to hear Mr. Brink bawling out his secretary. In a loud voice he said, "You idiot! You might have guessed that those girls were friends of Evelyn Starr's."

"I did try to get rid of them," Miss Dow defended herself. "You're the one who spoiled it by walking in here, and I expect you to apologize for calling me an idiot!"

"Oh, all right. I'm sorry," Mr. Brink said. "But there are times when you're no help to me at all. Don't you realize that the driver of that car, Moss Engels, doesn't want to lose his license?" Brink laughed. "Besides, that kid is loaded with money, and money talks!"

"How about that guy on the other side of Evelyn Starr? Is he ready to swear that the girl yanked the wheel away from Engels and actually drove the car into the tree?"

There was a short pause. "Eric Reese will do whatever Engels tells him to do," Mr. Brink responded. "We have no worry on that score."

"And the people in the back seat?" Miss Dow asked.

The lawyer said that this matter was already taken care of, but did not explain. "So you see, my dear Miss Dow, that of the three in the front seat there are now two to one against Evelyn Starr. Her word won't count. She doesn't stand a ghost of a chance."

Louise and Jean had heard enough to assist Evelyn, and they decided to leave before they were caught. Quickly they tiptoed along the hall and hurried down to the street.

When they were seated in their car once more,

"Let's listen for a clue!"

Jean said, "What do you think we should do next?"

Louise suggested that they go back to the hospital and try to find out exactly where Moss Engels and Eric Reese were. When they inquired at the desk, the woman said she was sorry but she could not help them. "I have no idea which hospital they were taken to."

As the girls walked out, Jean remarked, "The police will surely know. Let's contact them."

Louise stopped. "First, why don't we go back to see Evelyn? We can tell her we have evidence to prove her innocence."

"Good idea," Jean agreed.

When they reached Evelyn's room, they found that she was asleep and decided not to disturb her. Louise took a note pad from her purse and wrote a message, which she laid on their friend's night stand. Then she and Jean left the hospital.

The next stop was police headquarters, where they were cordially received. To their inquiry about where Moss Engels and Eric Reese were, the captain said, "At Mercy Hospital in Kirkland. Quite a ride from here. I'd say at least twenty miles."

The girls thanked him for the information and walked outside.

"I guess," said Louise, "that since the drive will be a long one, we'd better stop at the motel and tell Aunt Harriet where we're going."

"That's right," Jean agreed. "She'll worry anyway if we don't show up pretty soon."

As the sisters rode toward the Starfish, Jean said, "I hope Aunt Harriet won't forbid us to go. I'm not ready to give up sleuthing for the day. Why don't we ask her to ride over to Mercy Hospital with us before visiting hours are over?"

"Great!" Louise exclaimed.

She pulled their car up to one side of the curved driveway at the motel's main entrance and parked it behind a red sports car.

"That's Sally Benson's, isn't it?" Louise asked.

"Looks like it," Jean remarked.

As the girls walked into the lobby, they heard great excitement. The participants in the contest were talking excitedly and two were crying nervously.

"What can any of us do?" the girl who had performed effortless cartwheels asked another young woman.

Her friend choked back tears from her reddening eyes. "We've got to do something right away," she replied, "or Mrs. Menken may have to cancel the contest!"

The other said quickly, "I don't even want to be in it any more. Do you?"

The Danas were bewildered by the comments of contestants. What crisis had befallen the wonderful pageant?

"I wonder what has happened?" Louise remarked. "Judy Irish is beside herself."

At this moment Aunt Harriet, who had seen her nieces come in, hurried toward them. They asked her what the trouble was.

"Has somebody been injured?" Jean said.

"I hate to tell you this," Aunt Harriet replied, "but Sally Benson has disappeared!"

CHAPTER VI

Another Disappearance

"DISAPPEARED!" Louise and Jean cried out.

"Where? When? Aunt Harriet, don't keep us in suspense!" Louise begged.

Miss Dana said the desk clerk had revealed that Sally had come to him a little while earlier, asking for her mail. He had given her a letter, and she had walked to the elevator.

"After that, no one seems to have seen her," Aunt Harriet went on. "Everybody has been questioned, even the parking-lot attendant. No one saw Sally come out of the motel or leave in her car."

"We just spotted it parked outside," Jean said.

"Mr. and Mrs. Benson aren't here, so Sally couldn't have gone with them," Aunt Harriet told her nieces.

"How about Judy?" asked Jean. "Does she know anything about Sally's disappearance?"

"She said Sally left their room to get the mail. She planned to come right back, but never did."

"How long ago did she leave?" Louise asked.

"An hour or so."

The three Danas walked off by themselves to a small vacant area. All of them were upset by the news. Louise and Jean decided to try to find Sally at once.

"But where do we begin?" Jean asked.

Louise said she was sure the letter Sally had received had a direct bearing on her disappearance. She went to ask the desk clerk if he had noticed where it had come from, but he shook his head.

When Louise returned, Jean was saying, "I have a hunch that Sally planted the letter some place as a clue to us so we could find her!"

Louise agreed. Both girls thought that if Sally had left the motel quickly, she would probably have hidden the message in the lobby. They began a minute search, peering into every conceivable hiding place. Their starting point was the elevator door. Louise took the left side of the room, Jean the right.

As Louise approached the front entrance, she stopped to search among clusters of white artifical flowers in a large Asiatic vase. Jean caught up with her, admitting defeat.

Louise said excitedly, "I just found a letter!"

The envelope had no sender's name or address

and the stamp looked like an old one that had been pasted on. Just Sally's name, the motel and its address were written on the envelope.

Quickly Louise took out the letter and the two girls read it together.

Dear Miss Benson:

There is a plot to kidnap you some night soon. Right now it is safe for you to come to the parking lot to car CYR-991 for more information. Tell nobody.

Wing

The two Danas stared at each other. The same thought had popped into their minds. On the strange invitations they had received, the young sleuths had found a W and a G.

"Let's go upstairs and look at the invitations again," Jean urged. "We can see if an I and an extra N are ringed."

Aunt Harriet had already gone to her room. When the girls arrived, they showed her the note. "Don't you think you should hunt for Sally before you puzzle over these invitations?" she said.

Louise revealed that she had already checked with the desk clerk. "He said the parking-lot attendant had not seen Sally outside. But I'll call up the attendant and ask him to look for an automobile with the license-number CYR-991."

She did this while Jean started to work on the invitations. Presently she exclaimed, "I found another ringed N!"

"Great!" Louise said. She now inspected one of the invitations letter by letter, and even took out a small magnifying glass from her suitcase.

Presently she spotted a ringed I.

Aunt Harriet asked, "Have you any idea who Wing might be, or what it might stand for?"

Both girls said no, but Jean added, "It could be a Chinese person's name."

"Yes," Louise added. "And he could be in league with Charlie Ching."

Aunt Harriet suggested that Wing might be a symbol for something or even a code word. The girls agreed, but were more inclined to think it was the name of the person who had written the note to Sally and all the extra invitations as well.

Louise proposed that before trying to figure out the words the unused W and X made up, she and Jean see if they could pick up any clues about Sally outdoors. The first person they spoke to was the parking-lot attendant. He introduced himself as Perry and told them he had just started working there. Perry said no car with the license number CYR-991 was in the lot. Also, he had seen no one walking or running from the motel entrance to a car and driving off.

"I was thinking, though," he added, "that maybe

I did see the girl after all. I just caught a glimpse of a couple in a car as it left. She was very beautiful—I believe the most beautiful girl I've ever seen. I was so busy looking at her that I didn't notice who was driving or the license number."

"That's too bad," Jean remarked. "I'm sure it was Sally Benson you saw."

"Is she one of the contestants?" the young man asked.

"Yes."

Perry laughed. "If this were a beauty contest, she'd sure win it!"

"And she has a gorgeous singing voice," Louise added.

"Oh boy!" the young man exclaimed. "What a girl!"

Louise thanked him for the information and the Danas went back inside the motel. They were just in time to meet Mrs. Menken. The girls took her to a corner and showed her the note Louise had found among the flowers.

After reading it, the pageant chairman said, "This whole thing is dreadful. I don't know which way to turn. What do you suggest?"

Louise replied, "Call the police. They can put out an alarm and will have the license number to go by."

Mrs. Menken agreed and went at once to a telephone. As soon as the conversation was over, she summoned all the girls who were to be in the contest and asked them whether they knew of any reason for Sally's disappearance.

No one had any helpful information to offer, not even her roommate, Judy. Sally's disappearance remained a mystery, and Jean and Louise were baffled by it.

Louise asked Judy and the other girls if any of them knew a person named Wing.

"I know of one," Judy replied. "It's the nickname of a hockey player. I think his full name is Sam Wingsan."

"Is he Chinese?" Jean asked.

"Yes," Judy answered, "but Wing was born in this country. I've seen him play. He's a great guy!"

"Have you any idea where he is this summer?" Louise asked.

Judy thought a moment, then replied, "I believe his team is practicing far north in Canada."

Louise and Jean looked at each other. The hockey player could not possibly be Sally's kidnapper, assuming she had been abducted.

Mrs. Menken announced to the contestants that there would be no session that evening because of what had happened. The nineteen girls had no sooner left for their rooms, than the police arrived.

Mrs. Menken asked Louise and Jean to go with her to talk with them. The two officers were given full details. Mrs. Menken requested that all information be kept from the public because of the approaching pageant.

"When you get any clues, pass them on to the Dana girls," she said. "They have been very helpful so far in trying to solve this puzzling situation."

Before the officers left, Louise asked them if they had received any news about the people in the car accident. "The one in which our friend Evelyn Starr was injured," Jean added.

"Nothing, except that the two boys in the front seat are recovering. The couple in the rear of the car were not injured, and went to their homes," one of the officers told them.

By this time Louise, Jean, and Aunt Harriet were ready for a late dinner at the motel. During the meal they talked of nothing but the two mysteries they were trying to solve.

The next afternoon the Danas decided to drive to Mercy Hospital in Kirkland to see Moss Engels and Eric Reese.

"I'd like to find out whether the boys engaged Mr. Brink's services or he offered to take Engels' case," Louise said.

Jean tossed her head. "I'll bet he went to them and made the suggestion. He seems just like that kind of guy."

Aunt Harriet and her nieces went to the parking lot. They walked to the slot where they had left their car. It was not there!

The sisters looked all over the area. Not seeing their automobile, they appealed to the attendant, Perry.

"Did you move our car?" Louise asked him.

"Why no! Isn't it where you left it?"

"No."

Perry was worried. Here were the same girls who had asked him what had happened to Sally Benson! He looked around the parking lot, and shook his head anxiously.

There was silence for a few seconds, then Jean burst out, "Our car has been stolen!"

CHAPTER VII

Taxi Chase

THE three Danas looked at one another, nonplussed. Their car stolen!

Jean's face grew red with anger. "Everything and everybody is missing!" she cried.

Aunt Harriet put an arm around her niece's shoulders. "Don't take it so hard," she said soothingly. "I'm sure the police can find our car for us. I'll phone them."

"But the inconvenience!" Louise said. She, too, felt frustrated.

Miss Dana suggested that they get a cab. "That is," she added, "if you still want to go to the hospital to see those boys."

Both girls said they were eager to talk to them, but taking a cab would be expensive.

"Maybe not," Aunt Harriet replied. "Let's ask at the desk what the rates are. Anything within reason that will help others is not too expensive."

The three went inside and learned that the taxi rate to Kirkland and back was not exorbitant. The clerk asked, "Would you like me to call a cab for you?"

"Please do," Aunt Harriet answered. "And also contact the police. Our car has been stolen!" She gave him the necessary data.

"That's too bad," he said.

Within ten minutes the taxi arrived, and Aunt Harriet and her nieces climbed into the rear seat. The driver was a pleasant young man who chatted about various local affairs as they were riding toward Kirkland.

"I hear one of the contestants has disappeared," he said.

The Danas were startled that he knew about it. "Where did you hear that?" Louise asked him.

"Oh, it's all over town," he replied with a laugh. "People are wondering if she's a bride by this time."

"Oh no!" Jean exclaimed. "She would never do a thing like that. She was too keen about the contest. Have you heard anything else?"

The driver, according to the license and picture pasted on the back of the front seat, was named Harry Booker. He said, "Some people think she's been kidnapped, but no one's heard of any reason for it or demand for a ransom."

Aunt Harriet spoke. "Isn't it a little early for that?"

Harry said, "It doesn't take gossip long to get started." He laughed.

When they reached Mercy Hospital in Kirkland, the three Danas went inside. They learned there was only enough time left to visit one patient, so they chose Eric Reese.

Since the number of visitors was limited to two, Aunt Harriet offered to wait for the girls. Louise and Jean took the elevator and soon found Eric's room. They quickly introduced themselves and said they were friends of Evelyn Starr's.

"We haven't much time to talk," Louise explained. "Evelyn has been wondering how you're feeling."

Eric said he was somewhat better, but still bruised and shaken up by the accident. This was just the opening the girls had hoped to hear.

Jean asked, "Eric, did you really see Evelyn yank the wheel away from Moss Engels and let the car run into a tree?"

A frightened look came over Eric's face. Finally he replied, "I'm going to tell you the truth. I don't really know what happened, but I did not see Evelyn touch the wheel, and I'm sure she didn't."

Louise said they had gone to see Mr. Brink, the lawyer who was demanding that Evelyn take full responsibility for the accident and the consequences. "Mr. Brink told us he has your sworn testimony."

Eric replied shakily, "I didn't want to do it, but

Moss and Mr. Brink made me! I was too sick to refuse."

As the visitors' bell rang, the girls shook hands with Eric.

Louise said, "We must go now, but I'd like to tell you something. We want to be friends and advise you to have nothing more to do with either Moss Engels or Aaron Brink."

"I promise." Eric smiled. "You girls are great! I feel so much better. I knew the whole thing was wrong, but couldn't figure how to get out of it."

Jean said, "If you have any more trouble, get in touch with us at the Starfish Motel in Newport Beach."

"Thanks, I will."

When the girls reached the lobby, they sat down with their aunt. Louise told her what Eric had promised, and she was delighted.

"Your good deed for the day," she teased. "And now we must leave."

"I suggest," said Louise, "that we not discuss this case in the taxi. Harry seems to be quite a talker."

The three Danas laughed, but Louise became sober again. "One thing worries me—Evelyn is not yet clear of this case. Moss Engels apparently is still in league with Aaron Brink."

"You're right," her sister agreed. "I wonder what we should do next."

Louise had a suggestion. "I believe we should try to get in touch with Evelyn's brother, Franklin. Even if he's on a secret mission in China, somebody must know where he is."

Aunt Harriet nodded. "The State Department, probably," she told her nieces. "If you like, I'll contact them Monday and find out what I can. They may not tell me where Franklin Starr is, but might be willing to deliver a message."

Louise suggested that perhaps in the meantime there was someone else who might help them. "Professor Charles Ching." She looked at her watch. "Perhaps we could stop for just a few minutes at the Chings'. What do you all say?"

The other two voted for the idea, and when they got into the cab, directed Harry Booker to drive them there.

"Then we'll go back to town a different way," the taximan said.

He took them on a secondary road with little traffic. About a mile out of town, they saw a car ahead that was going rather slowly. As they neared it, Louise grabbed Jean's arm.

"Look! That car! It's ours!"

Aunt Harriet pointed out that it had a different license-plate number.

"The thief could have changed the plate," Jean reminded her.

Louise said excitedly, "You see that unpolished

spot on the left rear fender? I noticed it the first day."

By this time Harry had become interested. He asked, "You're sure that's your stolen car?"

"Positive!" Louise replied.

"You want me to chase it?" he asked.

"Oh yes!" the two girls cried out.

Harry put on speed and came alongside the other car. He got so close that the driver had to pull over to the edge of the road. By now he realized what was happening and he pressed the gas pedal.

He pulled ahead, but Harry was right after him. He kept forcing the other driver to the side. Though he never touched the other automobile, he brought his taxi close enough to keep the suspect at the edge of the pavement.

The chase went on. Jean bounced up and down in her seat and urged Harry to go faster.

"Cut him off! Cut him off!" she shouted.

Harry said he was hoping for a level stretch so that he could run the other man off the road, but the street became narrower, and there was a deep ditch on the right side.

The suspect kept pace and every so often would pull a few feet ahead. Harry was leaning forward, his arms around the steering wheel and his head bent low.

Aunt Harriet had kept quiet until now, but she finally called out, "We must stop this! It's too dangerous for all of us! That other driver may go into the ditch at any moment and turn over. And he may not be the thief at all! He may have bought that car innocently!"

"No such thing, ma'am," Harry explained. "If he were not guilty, he would have stopped long ago. Don't worry. I used to be a racing driver, and I know how to cut him off and get your car back for you!"

CHAPTER VIII

Police Sirens

THE race continued. Harry Booker seemed to be enjoying himself immensely. The cab driver started once to cut off the other driver.

Aunt Harriet screamed. "Don't do that!" she cried out. "We'll all be killed!"

"But we can't let that thief get away!" he told her, and went on at breakneck speed.

Louise and Jean became frightened. The race now was foolhardy. It seemed evident that neither the thief nor their driver would give up.

Louise leaned forward and tapped Harry on the shoulder. "Why don't you just stay behind the car?" she said.

Her plea fell on deaf ears. Harry set his jaw, pulled close to the other driver, and shouted at him to give up. Whether or not the man would have done so of his own volition was questionable, but at that moment they heard a police siren. The car with the revolving light on top was coming toward them from the rear.

Harry Booker mumbled something and finally slowed down. The vehicle in front of him stopped abruptly. The driver slid across the front seat, opened the door, and jumped out. He ran up a driveway to a farmhouse and disappeared in the darkness.

By this time the police car had reached the group. Two officers got out and walked over to the taxi.

"What's going on?" one of the men asked.

"Do you know how fast you were speeding?" the other added. "And what was the idea of trying to shove that other car off the road?"

Harry said, "I was trying to catch a thief!"

Louise and Jean, who had jumped out of the cab, confronted the officers. Between them they managed to make the men understand what had happened.

"The other automobile's empty," one of the policemen stated. "Where's the thief?"

The girls pointed toward the dark driveway. "He jumped out and ran that way. We never got a good look at the man's face, so we can't describe him."

Before the officers would accept the story, they asked many questions about where the Danas lived, and what they were doing in this area. Aunt Harriet leaned out of the cab window and told them.

"Dana? Dana?" said one of the policemen, who was Officer Heeber. "That name is familiar." He pulled out a notebook. "Yes, here it is. You reported a stolen car. What is your license number?"

Louise took the registration card from her purse and showed it to him. "The plates that are on the car now must have been put there by the thief," she said.

Officer Heeber turned toward his colleague. "I guess they're telling the truth," he said.

Jean asked, "May we take our car back to Newport Beach?"

"Yes, but not without the right plates," he replied.

Louise interrupted. "Let's see if they're hidden someplace in the car."

Everyone joined in the search, pulling out cushions, lifting the carpeting and examining the engine area. Meanwhile, the two officers had unlocked the trunk of the car and were busy rummaging among the extra tire, cleaning cloths in a sack, and a picnic hamper.

"I've found them!" Heeber called. He pulled first one, then the other, plate from beneath the picnic hamper. He smiled as he started to unbolt the fake plates.

"That's wonderful!" Jean exclaimed.

When the Danas' plates had been put on, Heeber told the girls and their aunt that they were free to go. The other officer added, "I'll report this by radio. But if you're stopped on the way home because you're driving a stolen car, tell the officers to get in touch with us." He pulled a card from his pocket and handed it to Louise.

Heeber turned to Harry Booker. "Since you were doing a good deed, which fortunately turned out to be one, I won't write out a ticket. But I do want to give you a warning: don't try to play policeman again!"

Harry promised not to do so. The officers said good-by and drove up the driveway to the farm, apparently to hunt for the thief.

Louise went to their car to be sure there was a reasonable amount of fuel in the tank. "Okay," she said. "We can leave now."

Aunt Harriet glanced at the taxi meter. She opened her purse and paid the fee, giving Harry a large tip. "We appreciate everything you did," she said. Then, smiling, she added, "Even if you did scare me half to death."

Harry said he was sorry about this. "I hope they find the thief and punish him. Maybe that will make up for it. Thank you very much for the tip. It will come in handy."

He drove off and waved to the Danas as they walked over to their own car. Soon they were on their way to Newport Beach.

Aunt Harriet said, "It's far too late to call on Professor Ching. Louise, please drive direct to the motel."

The parking-lot attendant looked at them in amazement. "You got your car back?" he asked.

Jean described their little adventure, and the young man's eyes opened wide. "You drove with Harry Booker, the former racing driver?"

"Yes, we did," Aunt Harriet replied. "And what a ride! I never want another one like it!"

When the Danas walked into the lobby of the motel, they were met by Judy Irish. She rushed up to them and said that Sally's parents had arrived.

"They're terribly upset, of course," Judy remarked. "I hope you don't mind, but I told them you are amateur sleuths and are trying to find Sally."

"No, of course not," Jean said. "Well, good night. See you in the morning."

Soon after church the following day, they met Judy again. While they were talking, a tall, good-looking couple approached the group. Judy introduced them as Mr. and Mrs. Benson.

They shook hands with the Danas, then Mrs. Benson said, "We came as soon as we heard the dreadful news. A few minutes ago Mr. Benson was in touch with the police again. Apparently there are no clues to Sally's whereabouts, and we have heard nothing about a ransom."

The three Danas expressed their sympathy, then told what little they knew about Sally's disappearance. Louise still had the note signed "Wing" in her bag, and turned it over to the Bensons.

She told them about the stolen car and their exciting adventure retrieving it. "I wonder if the man who took it is connected with this person Wing or a pal of his."

An answer to her remark was forestalled by the appearance of Mrs. Menken. She introduced herself to Mr. and Mrs. Benson and said she was dreadfully sorry about what had happened.

"Evidently Sally went off because she wanted to," Mrs. Menken said, "but I cannot guess her reason." She announced that rehearsals would proceed as if Sally were there. Then she hurried off.

In a few minutes the Bensons left the motel. Judy said there was to be a rehearsal at ten o'clock the next morning. Would Louise and Jean like to come to it? "This would be a chance for you to continue your individual interviews with the girls."

"Oh yes," Louise replied.

Monday morning at ten the Dana girls hurried off to the large room, where music was already being played. They sat down and watched as the contestants paraded. The Danas were fascinated by the intricate twists and turns and wondered if the girls were to be given points on their ability to perform this part of the ceremony.

One girl stood out among the others. Her name was Amalie Sung. She was from South Korea. At present she was a student in the United States and had entered the pageant from her college nearby.

"Isn't she beautiful?" Louise whispered to Jean.

"That gorgeous black hair and those lovely grayish-brown eyes!"

Jean nodded. "And what an exquisite complexion!" she said in a low tone. "Next to Sally, I'd say she's the best-looking one among the girls."

Louise agreed. "I wonder what her talent is." She said that if Amalie's cultural standing and talent matched the girl's looks and her perfect posture she would have a good chance to win.

Suddenly Jean sucked in her breath. "Do you think Sally's kidnapping could have anything to do with the competition? I mean, no one could beat her, except possibly Amalie."

"That's an idea, Jean, but it only complicates our case."

When the rehearsal was over, the Danas made a point of speaking to Amalie. At first she was a bit aloof. The South Korean girl became enthusiastic, however, when they mentioned that she must be happy about an Asiatic theme for the contest.

"It is a most delightful idea!" Amalie said. "You will like my costume when I show my talent." She did not say what it was, and the Danas did not inquire.

Louise asked, "By any chance do you know a man named Wing?"

Amalie shook her head. "No, I do not. He must be Chinese. Except for Professor Ching I do not know any other one in this area."

After the Danas got to their bedroom, Louise said, "That clue really faded out."

"It certainly did," Jean agreed.

The following day, when Jean woke, she saw Louise at work at the desk. In front of her were the puzzling invitations.

"Good morning, sis," Jean said cheerily, getting out of bed. "Boy, you're up early this morning."

Louise turned and gave a little shriek of delight. "I figured out some more letters!"

Jean came to her side. "What did you find?"

Louise showed her the new letters. "Here they are: P, H, O, E."

"What else goes with it?" Jean asked. "By itself it doesn't make any sense."

Her sister smiled. "How about Phoenix?"

Jean looked puzzled. "It sounds great, but what does it mean?"

CHAPTER IX

The Green Poison

THE two girls stared at the strange sentence, then Louise made a guess. "*Phoenix stolen crown wing.*"

Jean giggled. "Phoenix is a mythological bird. It has wings. Maybe the stolen crown is under one wing."

Louise chuckled. "Perhaps the bird flew away and we'll never find the valuable crown." Then she became serious again. "Let's assume there's only one word, a verb, missing."

"And that it is a short one," Jean said. "Why don't we try several three-letter words without hunting for them in the invitations? As a matter of fact, it might be in the one that Applecore burned."

The two girls assumed that Phoenix referred to a mythological bird. Jean suggested that they try "sit."

Louise burst out laughing. "Maybe it's a command and says, *'Phoenix, sit stolen crown wing!'* "

"Maybe it's 'sat,' " Louise suggested.

" *'Phoenix sat stolen crown wing.'* "

Her sister remarked that birds lay eggs. "Let's try 'lay.' *'Phoenix lay stolen crown wing.'* "

This sent Louise into peals of laughter. "It gets worse all the time."

Before they had a chance to think of any more three-letter words, Aunt Harriet walked into their room. "Good morning," she said. "I heard you giggling in here. What's the joke?"

When the girls told her about the funny sentence, she laughed too. Then she said, "Let me try."

After a momentary pause, she said, "How about *'Phoenix has stolen crown, Wing.'* "

"That sentence makes sense," Jean told her. "Now tell us what it means!"

"That's easy," Aunt Harriet teased. "You know Mrs. Menken has a crown. Probably this sentence refers to that."

"After breakfast, let's go to Mrs. Menken's house," Louise proposed.

Just then there was a knock on the door. Louise opened it to find one of the porters holding out a cablegram.

"Is your aunt in here?" he asked. "She didn't answer my knock on her door."

"Yes," Louise replied. "I'll give her the cablegram."

Aunt Harriet had come toward the porter, purse in hand. She opened it and gave him some change.

He said thank you, then went off. She closed the door.

"Is it from Uncle Ned?" Louise asked.

Aunt Harriet said she doubted this. "I was expecting a cablegram from someone else."

As she opened the envelope, the girls wondered whom she meant. A broad smile crossed Miss Dana's face. "This is from Franklin Starr," she announced. "I was doing a little detective work on my own."

"Tell us about it, and what does the cable say?" Jean asked.

Aunt Harriet said that she had contacted the State Department, which had been very understanding and promised to get in touch with Evelyn's brother immediately.

"The message is, 'Will leave China at once and come direct to Newport Beach.'"

Jean and Louise were delighted. They both hugged Aunt Harriet and danced around the room with her.

"You're wonderful!" Jean sang out.

"And a great detective!" Louise added. "I think we should phone Evelyn and tell her at once."

The others agreed, and Louise called the hospital. The squeal of delight that echoed over the phone was quite audible.

"Oh, I'm so relieved!" Evelyn said. "How did you darling people ever get in touch with him?"

Louise told her and added, "I'm sure this is going to make you get well in a hurry!"

Suddenly Evelyn became serious. "It should," she said, "but I'll tell you something disturbing. Last night Mr. Brink came to the hospital to see me.

"He said he was not going to change his charge against me. I was tempted to say that I was no longer worried, when he said, 'Tell those Dana girls that if they don't stop their snooping, I will make it hot for them!' "

"Oh dear!" Louise said. But quickly she went on, "Evelyn, we think Mr. Brink is bluffing. Please don't let him upset you. Jean and I will watch our step. We promise. Anyway, your brother will be here soon, and he'll take care of the whole matter. Please don't worry!"

The injured girl finally said, "All right. I'll try not to. But you must be very, very careful. Keep in touch with me, so I know you're all right."

Directly after breakfast Louise telephoned Officer Heeber at the state trooper headquarters and asked if the thief who had stolen the Dana car had been apprehended.

"No, not yet," he responded.

She asked, "Do you think the thief could be identified by the old plates he was using?"

The officer told her they were counterfeit, so there would be no way of tracing the number.

Louise was amazed. She said, "So this is a new racket."

"I'm afraid so," Heeber said.

When Louise reported the conversation to Jean, she sighed. "Another clue washed out. What do you think we should tackle now?"

Louise thought they should go to Mrs. Menken's home and tell her the sentence they had figured out from the invitations. The chairman of the pageant was surprised to see the girls, but ushered them in graciously.

"I know you've brought some exciting news. Otherwise you would have phoned for an appointment."

When Louise showed her the piece of paper on which the possible message was written, Mrs. Menken was puzzled.

"I have no idea what it might mean. I'm sure you have already guessed the answer."

Louise shook her head. "Unfortunately we haven't, but we do have two clues. We believe that Wing is a person, and we know that your original crown was stolen. But that's as far as we can go at this time."

The girls were disappointed that Mrs. Menken could not furnish any further clue.

"May we look again at the crown in the cabinet?" Jean asked.

"Certainly."

The sisters followed her to the other room, and once more she unlocked the cabinet.

"Let's study this crown thoroughly," Louise suggested.

Mrs. Menken lifted the headdress out and set it on a table. She and the Dana girls began to finger it. They were so intent on their work, that it was several minutes before they noticed the condition of their hands.

"Look!" Jean exclaimed suddenly. "Our hands are turning green!"

Mrs. Menken's were quite stained, and Louise's were worst of all.

"We'd better wash this off immediately," the woman said, and ran toward a powder room. "You girls use this basin. I'll go to the kitchen," she said.

Warm soapy water soon removed the stain entirely from Jean's hands, but Louise's still showed hints of green. Again she washed them with fresh water and more soap. Mrs. Menken joined them, her own hands perfectly clean.

Louise lifted hers out of the water and dried them thoroughly. The discoloration had disappeared, but her hands were swelling visibly!

"Oh dear!" Mrs. Menkin cried out. "I'm going to call my doctor and ask him what we should do. This might be poison!"

In a few minutes she was back with instructions. "Louise, Dr. Allen said you should pour gasoline over your hands. Wipe them off immediately. Then you should soak them in plain cold water. As soon as the swelling has gone down, I'll get you some soothing hand cream."

"What did the doctor say happened to us?" Louise asked.

"That probably there was poison on the crown. If this treatment doesn't work, we're to call him again."

She told Jean where to find a small can of gasoline near the door in the garage. "Please get it."

Jean was out the door in a jiffy. She grabbed the container and returned to the house. As Louise held her hands over the basin, Jean covered them thoroughly with the liquid.

"Don't leave it on too long," Mrs. Menken advised.

Jean was already running cold water into the basin. Louise immersed her hands. Within five minutes the onlookers could see a change. The puffiness in Louise's fingers was actually disappearing!

"Thank goodness nothing worse happened to you," Mrs. Menken said.

Louise smiled. "And I'm glad we found out about the crown before it was set on the head of the pageant winner!

Jean tossed her head. "I'd like to get hold of the

"Look! Our hands are turning green!"

villain who put that poisonous powder on the crown! I suppose he did it to keep from being found out as a thief. Mrs. Menken, do you think it would be a good idea to have a chemist find out what it is?"

The woman agreed. She said she would put on heavy gloves, then scrape off some of the powder into an envelope. "I'll take it downtown at once."

As Mrs. Menken did this and drove off, the girls got into their own car. Louise turned away from the road to town. Jean asked where she was going.

"To Professor Ching's," her sister replied. "I want to learn all I can about the Phoenix."

Jean said she had read that the mythological bird could consume itself with its own fire. "From the ashes will come a beautiful young bird," she said. "The Phoenix was reputed to live five or six hundred years."

"I'm sure Professor Ching will know more about the story of the Phoenix than that," Louise said. "The only thing that's worrying me right now is that the word Phoenix may not refer to a bird at all. It could mean the city in Arizona."

Jean gave a heavy sigh. "I thought we were coming nearer the solution. Are you saying we might have to start all over again?"

CHAPTER X

Chinese Birthday

Professor and Mrs. Ching greeted Jean and Louise cordially. Both were dressed up, and the girls wondered if they were going out.

"If you're just leaving, we'll come back some other time," Louise told them.

"No," said Mrs Ching, "but we are having a special luncheon and would like it very much if you would join us."

"Oh, we don't want to interrupt a party," Jean said quickly.

Professor Ching smiled. "It is a very private party, with only Madame Ching and myself. You would do us a great honor by staying."

Both girls accepted the invitation. "I'm very glad," said Mrs. Ching. "A surprise will be served. I would like you to try it."

Louise and Jean were curious to know what the

treat was, but were too polite to ask. If Mrs. Ching wanted them to know ahead of time, she would tell them.

The lovely Chinese woman excused herself and went to the kitchen. Professor Ching and the girls sat down in the living room to talk.

"May I call our Aunt Harriet and tell her where we are?" Louise asked him.

"Please do so. There is a telephone in the hall."

When Louise returned, Jean was just finishing a story she had read concerning the Phoenix. "That's all I know about the mythological bird," she concluded. "Could you tell us anything more?"

The elderly man smiled. "Probably the most exciting story regarding the Phoenix is an old Chinese legend. It is said that wherever the bird may light, a treasure can be found buried underneath."

The Danas laughed, and Louise said, "That's a great story." She now told the Professor how she and Jean happened to think of the word. They did not reveal, however, the whole message they had figured out.

Jean's eyes sparkled. "I'd like to find a buried treasure under some Phoenix!"

Professor Ching smiled at the girl's enthusiasm. "I suggest that you search for an artificial Phoenix and look underneath it. You may have great good luck."

He offered to show his callers a picture of the

mythological bird. They followed him to a book-case, where he took down one of the volumes. The professor laid the book on a table and opened it to a certain page.

"Here is a picture of a *Fang Huang* statue. That's the Chinese name for a Phoenix."

The bird was bright red. The tip of each wing was like twelve fingers, and its very long tail curled over the bird's head. The breast feathers ended in what seemed to be two stunted arms. Its legs were very skinny but the claws were long and wide.

"What a fantastic-looking creature!" Louise remarked. "Professor Ching, I notice that there is no artist's name."

"You are right," he agreed. "I checked the back of the book on the credits page, but the Phoenix was not mentioned. There was no reference to any place or museum where the statue of the bird might be seen."

"This is definitely a photograph," Jean remarked, "so there must be a bird like this some place."

Louise suggested they get in touch with the publisher of the volume and try to track down the photographer. She took a notebook from her bag and wrote down the name and address of the company.

At this moment Mrs. Ching returned and invited everyone to enter the dining room for lunch.

How attractive the low table was in its Asiatic

setting! Yellow and white flowers were artistically arranged in the center. Three-inch-high candles flickered in shallow decorative bowls. Low, comfortable cushions had been placed around the table and the Danas were assigned to two of them. The professor sat at one end, his wife, at the other.

The door from the kitchen swung inward and a pretty Asiatic girl, smiling broadly, entered with a tray of soup bowls. She was introduced to Louise and Jean as Mitzi Young from South Korea.

Professor Ching said, "Mitzi is studying at the university where I teach. She has agreed to serve us today because it is a celebration."

Mitzi acknowledged the introduction, but no one mentioned what the day or the luncheon was celebrating. The visitors looked around for a clue but could find none.

Mitzi set the bowls of soup in front of each one. Then, bowing to the host, she left the room.

Jean was thinking, "I can't eat soup with chopsticks, and there's no silver on the table. Am I supposed to pick this up and drink it?"

Politely she and Louise waited for their hostess to start. To their surprise, it was the professor who made the first move. "I'm afraid Mitzi forgot the ladles," he told his wife.

Mrs. Ching pressed a buzzer and Mitzi appeared. She instantly realized her error and went to get the ladles. They were wooden, with ornate, black-lacquered handles on which long blades of green grass had been painted.

It was egg-drop soup and delicious. No one made any remarks about the food. They spoke about the travels of Louise and Jean in various parts of the United States and foreign countries.

"Which one did you like best?" the professor inquired.

In one breath the two girls said, "Thailand." Louise added that she thought the country was fascinating, and the architecture of the temples and the gardens, superb.

The next course was *Moo Goo Gai Pan*. Somewhat like a delicious stew, it consisted of small pieces of pork, chicken, celery, pea pods, and a bowl of rice served separately. Mitzi passed around mild mustard and fragrant apricot sauces.

When it was time for dessert, she brought in four portions. In the center of each beautifully painted small plate lay a round piece of cake. The middle of it had been scooped out. In the depression was half of a very large peach. Apricot sauce had been poured over the top.

When everyone had been served, Mrs. Ching rose. She signaled, indicating that Louise and Jean should rise also. Following her lead, they all bowed to the professor, who was smiling broadly.

Mrs. Ching said, "This is the birthday of my kind and honorable husband. As our dessert suggests, may I wish you a long life and happiness."

Louise and Jean offered their congratulations and good wishes as well. After they sat down again, Mrs. Ching explained that this was the traditional birthday cake of ancient China and the custom of serving it was still observed.

"There is a story about its origin," she said. "There was once a peach tree that never died, but bore fruit only once every three thousand years."

"What a delightful story!" Louise remarked.

Jean added, "I'd hate to wait three thousand years to get a second peach!"

The others laughed, and Mrs. Ching said, "The myth said that only the gods could eat this fruit, so the peach became sacred to the peasants. I'm sure they ate the peaches they grew just the same, even though it was called the fruit of the gods."

Professor Ching thanked them all for their good wishes. "I will tell you another Chinese myth, which I think is most amusing. Once upon a time, up in the sky, there was an ox star. In ancient days most of the food people had to eat consisted of the animals they hunted. The result was that they ate only every three or four days, sometimes going longer between meals.

"The God of Heaven felt sorry for them, so he instructed the ox star to go down to earth and tell the people that the God of Heaven would see to it that they ate at least every three days.

"Now the ox star was rather stupid and when he delivered the message, he said that the God of Heaven wanted the people to know that he would see to it everybody ate three times a day. The God of Heaven was so angry with the ox star, he decided to punish him. So he sent the ox star to live on the earth permanently, where he would pull a plow, so that people could eat three times a day!"

Louise and Jean laughed. Both said they would like to learn more about Chinese mythology, and Professor Ching said he would give them one of his books on the subject.

"Oh, thank you," said Louise. "We promise to take very good care of it and return the book to you in excellent condition."

The professor's eyes twinkled. "I am Chinese, so anything I present is a gift. The book is for you to keep."

Again, Louise and Jean thanked him. He now rose from the table and the others followed him into the living room. He got the book and handed it to them.

After they left the house, Louise and Jean headed for the hospital to call on Evelyn. To their delight, she was sitting up near the window. Evelyn looked much better.

"I just can't wait for your visits," she said. "One minute I feel okay, then I start to think about that awful Mr. Brink and what he might do to me!"

"Please stop worrying," Louise begged her. "Once he finds out Eric Reese has told us the truth he'll reconsider. By that time your brother will have arrived."

Evelyn smiled. "You always know how to make me feel better," she said. Then she asked, "Is there any news about Sally?"

The Danas shook their heads. "Not unless some has come since we left the motel," Louise said. "We're going back to ask. If we hear anything exciting, I'll phone you."

When Louise and Jean reached the motel, they went at once to find Aunt Harriet. She wanted a report on the luncheon at the Chings'. Before telling her, Jean inquired about Sally. "Any word?"

"Unfortunately, no," Miss Dana answered.

Her nieces gave a full account of all they had seen and heard. Then Louise said, "I want to go up to my room and phone the publisher in New York who reproduced the photograph of the beautiful Phoenix."

The three went upstairs and Louise made the call. She spoke for nearly ten minutes with four different people at the firm before she was able to get the information. At first, the editor to whom she was speaking did not wish to reveal the photographer's name.

"It is very important that I find out," Louise said. "I'm helping to solve an international theft.

We think a Phoenix is involved and that the photographer might help us. If you think it's necessary, I can have the police chief here phone you."

The editor went off to consult someone else. Finally he returned and said, "The man is Mr. Braverman. At present he's on vacation."

Louise begged to know where.

"Oh, I guess there's no harm in telling you," the man said. "He's in Newport Beach at the Starfish Motel."

Louise could hardly believe the words she had heard. What a stroke of luck for the Danas!

CHAPTER XI

Unexpected Clues

LOUISE passed the interesting news on to Aunt Harriet and Jean. Both were delighted and said they could hardly wait to meet Mr. Braverman.

Jean picked up the phone and asked to be connected to the man's room. It rang several times, but there was no answer.

"Let's go downstairs and consult the desk clerk," Jean suggested.

Aunt Harriet thought the two girls should go together. "I want to finish some letters," she said, "so I'll beg off."

The sisters hurried away and asked at the desk where Mr. Braverman might be.

"I'll check with the manager," the young man replied and went to an inner office to get Mr. Smith. He smiled and said, "Do you just want to meet the famous Mr. Braverman, or is he part of your sleuthing?"

The girls grinned and admitted that he might provide a clue. Mr. Smith led them out of the motel to an attractive patio garden.

A tall, slender man with graying hair was reclining in a lounge chair, reading. As the visitors approached, he jumped up and smiled.

"Mr. Braverman, this is Louise Dana and her sister Jean. I must warn you that they are amateur detectives. They want to ask you some questions." Mr. Smith grinned.

The photographer laughed. "I've had many interviews, but none by two charming, attractive amateur sleuths. Please sit down."

The girls found him affable and he gave them a surprising answer about his picture credit of the Phoenix.

"The reason why I didn't put either the owner's name on the picture or my own was that he requested it."

Jean inquired whether the owner lived far from Newport Beach.

Mr. Braverman gazed at her intently, then said, "I guess it won't hurt if I say no to you. And I also think it wouldn't matter if I tell you that the man is of Asiatic background."

Louise asked if the owner of the Phoenix had other mementos of his native land in his home.

This time the photographer looked at her keenly. Finally he laughed. "If I tell you much more, I'm sure you'll be able to track down the man. But to answer you, yes, he has many Asiatic objects in his possession."

Louise and Jean glanced at each other, then Jean said, "By any chance, does he have an empress's crown?"

Mr. Braverman said no. "This time you didn't get a clue." He grinned.

Jean was ready with another question. "Would you mind telling me what the Phoenix is standing on?"

Again Mr. Braverman was amused. "The bird is perched on top of a black teakwood carved stand."

Suddenly Louise's eyes began to dance. "Mr. Braverman," she said, "what would happen to you if you told us the owner's name?"

"I could be ruined by a lawsuit," he replied.

Louise said she would not want this to happen and diplomatically changed the subject. She began talking about the upcoming pageant.

"Are you planning to attend?" she asked.

"Indeed, I am. As a matter of fact, that is why I came here. I am going to take pictures and write a story for a magazine."

He asked if Louise and Jean were going to appear in the contest.

"No," Louise said, "but we're to be teen-age judges."

Mr. Braverman shook his head. "I don't envy you your job. That's one of the hardest things to do, and somebody's feelings are bound to be hurt."

"Oh, I hope nothing like that happens!" Jean exclaimed.

"By the way," said Mr. Braverman, "I understand one of the contestants has disappeared mysteriously. What a great news story that is!"

Louise told him that everybody was trying to keep the information hush-hush, but she understood from the taxi driver that by now people in town knew about it.

"That's right," Mr. Braverman said.

Louise and Jean stood up to leave. Before saying good-by, Jean asked the man if he knew anybody called Wing.

The photographer shook his head. "No, I don't, but I understand that someone by that name submitted a manuscript on Asiatic art to my publisher. I was told he's a good artist but a poor writer. Anyway, his manuscript was not accepted."

"By any chance, does this Mr. Wing live nearby?" Louise wanted to know.

"I have no idea," Mr. Braverman replied. "Also, I don't know anything about his family or friends."

The two girls hurried back to their room and told Aunt Harriet what they had learned. "Now I'm sure," Louise added, "that in our mystery wing does not refer to the Phoenix. It's a man's name!"

Miss Dana wanted to know how they were going to pursue this clue, since Mr. Braverman had no idea where Mr. Wing lived.

Louise went to the telephone table and hunted

through the local listing. Presently she said, "There are three people in Newport Beach with the name Wing!"

Jean groaned. "Why didn't we think of looking there before? Who's the first one you're going to contact?"

Louise said the man had a laundry. "I think I'll skip him and try the second one."

When a woman answered, she asked if any member of her family was an artist. The response was no.

Louise put the phone down, then dialed another number. A woman with a sweet Asiatic accent answered.

Louise introduced herself, then asked, "Is anyone in your family an artist?"

"Yes," the woman replied. "He is my son, and he has disappeared! Have you any news about him?"

Louise was so excited to hear this that she could hardly reply. Finally she said, "I might have. I don't know. Can you tell me a little more about what happened?"

Mrs. Wing revealed that her son Peter had gone out on Friday afternoon, saying he would not be away long. "He has never come back or communicated with his father or me. We are dreadfully worried."

Friday! That was the day Sally had left!

Louise asked Mrs. Wing if he had mentioned where he was going, and if he had left by car.

"He didn't say, but he did take his car."

"What's the license number?" the girl detective queried.

"CYR-991."

"Then I do have some news for you," Louise told her. "One of the girls in our group at the Starfish Motel received a note signed Wing. It asked her to meet him in his car. The license number was the one you've just given me. Sally Benson has never returned either!"

Mrs. Wing gasped. "Oh, our son is a good boy. He would never abduct anyone. Something very wrong must have happened!"

By this time Mr. Wing, who had apparently overheard the conversation, came to the phone. He asked Louise to please identify herself a little further and tell him more about the girl who might have disappeared with their son Peter.

Louise gave him full details and told Mr. Wing that Sally Benson's parents were at the motel and were dreadfully worried.

Mr. Wing, who had a deep, pleasant voice, said, "You and your sister are amateur detectives, you say. What would you suggest we do? Get in touch with the police? We haven't done that in order to avoid embarrassment."

Louise told him the authorities had already been

notified, but so far had turned up no clues to the missing couple.

"I'm sure Sally didn't know your son. The only reason why she went to meet him was because of a strange message he sent. I think I should tell you this. The note to Sally said that she was going to be kidnapped some evening. If she would come to the car that afternoon, he would tell her more about everything."

Peter's father said in an even voice, "I guess there is no doubt about this Sally and our Peter having been kidnapped together!"

Mr. Wing went on to say that during the winter Peter attended college and was an exemplary student. He had tried to obtain a full-time position for the summer, but had failed. "Instead, Peter has been doing odd jobs for various people. His mother and I do not know the names of any of the persons for whom he worked."

"By any chance," said Louise, "did he ever mention a man named Mr. Ching?"

Peter's father said he was sorry but his son never had. He and Louise promised each other to telephone if either picked up a clue to the missing couple.

After Louise had hung up, the three Danas went over the whole case. Each clue and lead in the mystery was thoroughly discussed.

Finally Jean said, "I think our next move should

be to try to find Charlie Ching. I have a strong hunch he's in this area, even though he's not listed in the phone book."

Aunt Harriet suggested that they ask the police. To their disappointment but not surprise, the authorities said that if there were two Charles Chings in the area, they did not know about it.

"Now what?" Louise asked.

Miss Dana answered. "I think you girls need some relaxation. You've been working on this mystery day and night. Why not go down to the beach, take a dip, and then a nice sun bath?"

"That's a great idea!" Jean exclaimed. "We need to clear our heads and get some suntan. We've lost nearly all we had."

It did not take Louise and Jean long to put on their swimsuits, sandals, and robes. When they reached the beach, they were amazed to find it practically deserted. But in a few minutes they realized the probable reason.

Unsuspecting, the two sisters ran into the water and dived under a wave. They did not swim out far, because a terrific backwash followed each wave. Very soon they had had enough exercise and walked up onto the sand. In one spot children had evidently dug a large shallow pit.

"That's like a bed," Louise remarked. "And big enough for two."

She and Jean flopped face down into the depression, and soon were fast asleep. A little later both of them were awakened when a load of sand was dumped on top of them.

Instantly they struggled to get up. It was impossible! Try as they would, the girls found the weight too heavy to lift.

Louise and Jean panicked. They were buried under sand! And perhaps water too?

CHAPTER XII

Peculiar Footprints

NEARLY exhausted, Louise and Jean fought to get out from under the heavy wet sand. Neither girl could move any part of her body!

Louise thought, "I can't hold my breath much longer! I'll be smothered. And how is Jean?"

Her sister had the same concern, when suddenly she felt something touch her hand. It was another hand!

The strong fingers began to yank her arm. The movement hurt, but Jean realized that her whole body had edged sideways. Although it was only a fraction of an inch, the action had dislodged the heavy wet sand enough so she could move her other arm. Through her rescuer's efforts and her own, it was only another second before she could breathe again.

"Thank goodness you're alive!" a young man in swim trunks said.

Jean's first words were, "Thanks. Where's my sister?"

On the opposite side of the huge mound of sand, another swimmer was clawing at the thick cover over Louise. He had managed to reach one of her feet. Realizing that he must rescue her quickly before she became asphyxiated, the young man dug furiously where he thought her head was. Seconds later he felt her hair and scooped away the sand. The imprisoned girl managed to turn her face partly around and gulp in deep breaths of air.

Neither of the swimmers said a word. They used all their energy to dig at the sand until the two girls were released.

"Oh, thank you!" Louise said in a weak voice. "We were asleep. What happened to us?"

One of the swimmers said that as they came out of the water, they saw two men pulling a two-wheeled cart filled with wet sand.

"Suddenly they poured the whole load over you girls, then ran off with their cart."

"We got here as soon as we could," said the other young man, who told them his name was George. "And this is my friend Jerry. Were the men who dumped sand on you enemies of yours?"

"We don't know," Jean replied with a cough. "What did they look like?"

Jerry said, "The men were too far away from the water for us to see them clearly."

The swimmers helped the girls to the spot where they had left their robes. Louise and Jean felt sore and stiff. Both of them did a few calisthenics before being able to talk without puffing and hesitating.

"Tell me," said Jerry, "do you feel all right? Are you staying at the motel? We'll be glad to take you to your room."

"Thank you," Louise said. "But really, I feel fine now. How about you, Jean?"

Her sister smiled. "I'm beginning to believe I'm myself again. What's on your mind, sis?"

Louise said she would like to look around the beach. "Maybe we can pick up some clues to the men who tried to bury us." She asked the swimmers which way the men had gone with the cart.

George pointed south, and Jerry said, "I suppose you would like to search for tire tracks and footprints, but you won't find any. The men pulled the cart down to where the water was still coming in, so it washed away all footprints."

George added, "If you girls are feeling all right, then Jerry and I will hop off. We have dates tonight and must dress. Want us to report what happened to the police?"

"Oh, we'll do it," Louise said.

Both Danas thanked the young men again and Jean said impishly, "Have you ever rescued two girls out of a sand heap before?"

The boys shook their heads. "This is a first,"

George replied. "And I hope we don't have to repeat it. To tell you the truth, we were scared out of our wits."

"I guess we were afraid ourselves," Louise admitted.

After the two swimmers had left, Louise and Jean did find tire tracks leading down to the water, but any footprints their attackers might have left, had been obliterated. The two young sleuths kept on walking. Some five hundred feet farther on, they came to a fence. The cart, a type of dump wagon, had been left there. Nothing was inside it, and no mark of identification gave a clue to the owner's name.

"Well, we can cross off that lead," Jean said with a sigh.

Louise remarked, "Unless those men climbed the fence, they probably walked to the roadway. It runs in front of the various motels and private homes of Newport Beach."

With no particular plan in mind, the girls stepped up to the fence. Here, there were only two sets of footprints. At once Louise and Jean noticed that the right foot of one set was larger than the other, and had a strange set of toes. Some were small, some too large. Each varied in length from normal.

"That one doesn't even look real," Jean remarked. "I'll bet one of the men put an artificial foot over his own—you know the kind that are used as jokes."

"You might be right," Louise agreed. "Just the same, I think we should tell the police in case these are the prints of the two men who buried us."

The footmarks ended at the sidewalk. Since people in bathing suits were not allowed beyond this point, the Danas knew they would have to go back to their own beach. They glanced up and down, hoping to spot a policeman or anyone who might report the incident to the authorities, but no one was in sight.

The two girls returned to the motel beach and went to their room. Aunt Harriet was astounded by their story and advised her nieces to be particularly cautious while staying in Newport Beach.

"And please don't go to sleep again in a public place!" she begged.

"You can bet we won't," Jean answered.

Louise had already walked to the telephone and dialed police headquarters. The sergeant on duty was amazed at what she told him and said a man would immediately be sent to the spot where the footprints were.

"Please let me know," Louise requested, "if the prints are real or were made by someone wearing a funny flipper-type sandal."

The officer promised to do so. When Louise turned from the phone, Aunt Harriet said, "You girls had better change your clothes and hurry. Mrs. Menken is expecting you to attend a rehearsal of the contestants today. They're going to go through their talent show."

Her nieces ran to take showers and put on fresh summer pantsuits. Louise's was blue, Jean's yellow.

The Danas were amazed at the talent that was exhibited. Judy was superb in her acrobatic act. The applause from the other girls and the older judges who were there was long and enthusiastic.

One by one, the contestants performed their numbers. Each one seemed perfect. But the girl who received the most applause was Amalie, who played an original piano composition. She announced that it illustrated the difference between music of her native land, South Korea, and that of America during the same period. It was intriguing and ended with a grand finale.

The applause was tremendous, and when it was over Jean whispered to Louise, "There's no doubt in my mind now that if Sally doesn't show up before the pageant begins, Amalie will win first place."

Louise nodded. "I agree." She gave a great sigh. "The time left for finding Sally is very short."

The following morning Louise suggested to her sister that they call at the various shoe stores in Newport Beach and ask about a customer with strange-looking toes. They spent an hour at this bit of sleuthing, but learned nothing.

"Now what?" Jean asked.

Her sister was ready with an answer. "Let's find out about any podiatrists or foot doctors in town."

"Good idea," Jean said.

They went into a drugstore where there was a phone booth and a local directory.

"There's only one—a Dr. Snyder, who is a foot surgeon," Louise said, after checking the telephone book.

She drove to his office and parked. Inside, the Danas told the pleasant, young receptionist-nurse that they wished to see the doctor.

"I'm sorry," the girl said, "but he won't be in today."

"Then I guess we'll have to return some other time," Louise told her.

The young woman laughed nervously. "Can I help you? Of course, I can't operate on your feet, but if you just came for some information, I'm sure I could give it to you. I'm only here while the regular girl is on vacation, but I've learned a lot."

Louise and Jean were amused but thought this young woman was just the type who might tell them what they wanted to know.

Louise said, "Perhaps you can help us. We're most eager to gather more information about a certain man who came to see us, but we didn't meet him because we were asleep at the time."

"And you think he might be a patient of Dr. Snyder's?" the girl asked.

Jean said this was possible. "Our clue is that the man's right foot has very strange-looking toes."

"Oh, I know the very person you mean," the talkative nurse said. "He's Chinese. I don't remember his name offhand, but I can try to find it. The trouble is he always pays cash on his visits, so I never send a bill."

Louise's and Jean's hearts jumped. Were they really on the trail of the man who had tried to bury them alive and might also have stolen the priceless crown?

The young nurse rummaged through the files, but finally said, "No luck. Sorry."

Louise said slowly, "You say he's Chinese. Let's try some Chinese names, and you can look in your records for those. First try Ching."

The young woman did so. She shook her head. "No Ching here." Then suddenly she snapped her fingers. "But wait a minute. The doctor has a private file. Maybe that name's in there."

Louise and Jean did not feel this was an ethical thing for the girl to do, but before they could stop the nurse, she had spun through a swinging door and disappeared. She came back smiling.

"I found it. His name is Charles Ching. No address is given. But I remember now Dr. Snyder told me once that the man lived way out in the country on a big estate. He thought I might like to see it sometime. It was the second house from the boulevard on Shoreline Road. Would you know where that is?"

"No," Louise replied, "but I'm sure we could find it."

Both Danas thanked the nurse and left the place in high spirits.

"Let's get directions to Shoreline Road. I know where the boulevard is," Jean said.

The sisters were so excited that they grabbed each other's hand and ran toward their car.

CHAPTER XIII

Worrisome Moment

As Louise and Jean rode away from the foot doctor's office, Jean laughed.

"What's so funny?" her sister asked.

"Can you imagine," Jean said, "what Dr. Snyder would say if he knew his replacement nurse was going through his private file?"

Louise, grinning, replied, "My guess is that he'd be furious and give her a bawling out."

"Especially since she told the information to strangers," Jean added. "He should have locked his file and hidden the key."

Louise puckered her lips and said, "Maybe we have honest faces. Sometime I must take a good look at you, Jean."

By now she had reached the boulevard and wondered whether to turn left or right, toward Shoreline Road. Jean thought they should head for the beach, but Louise reminded her that the nurse had said Mr. Ching lived in the country.

"Maybe the shoreline cuts into that direction," she suggested. "Okay with you if I take a right?"

"Okay. I remember seeing a map of Newport Beach, and the shoreline did turn that way."

Louise drove another three miles. There was Shoreline Road!

"It's the second house from the boulevard," Louise said.

She slowed down, but found that the houses were far apart. They were surrounded by large estates. The girls went on for some distance until they came to one with high stone pillars at the entrance.

Louise stopped and the sisters stared first at the words on the left pillar, then at the one on the right.

"How odd!" Jean commented. "Those on the left look Chinese. *Shou-Lao.* I wonder what it means. And the one on the right sounds Italian. *Rizzo.*"

"This must be the place," Louise said. "Let's go in."

Jean hesitated. Her sixth sense told her they should be wary. She wondered whether Rizzo was the present or former owner, or did the word refer to something else?

"I have a strange feeling we might be walking into a trap," Jean said. "Let's drive a little farther and see if we can find the name Ching. That nurse may not have remembered exactly what the doctor said."

Louise agreed. The road ran down to the waterfront. Every estate had an identification, but none of them was Ching. Louise turned the car around and they headed back for the grounds with the pillars.

"We needn't go in," Louise said.

"Let's take a chance," Jean urged. "If things don't seem right, we'll stay out of the house."

As they were about to turn into the driveway, the sisters became aware of a small plane overhead. It was aimed in their direction!

"That pilot must be in trouble!" Louise exclaimed.

She put on power and shot between the entrance pillars. The plane changed course and headed toward them again.

Jean was excited. "He isn't in trouble! He's buzzing us!"

Louise edged ahead. The plane was not only coming lower, but definitely zeroing in on them! Didn't the pilot see them? Did he intend to hit them?

"That pilot doesn't want us here!" Louise cried out.

She made a wide sweep in the road, turned quickly, sped out into the main road and back toward the boulevard.

"That pilot doesn't want us here."

"Phew!" Jean said. She felt limp. "Louise, I'm sure you saved us from being killed!"

Louise had stopped the car. "I was scared out of my wits," she said. "My guess is that the pilot intended to land on the estate and didn't want us to see him or any passenger he might have had."

The two girls talked over the incident for some time. Louise reminded Jean that Evelyn's brother Franklin should be arriving soon.

"Maybe we should leave a visit to Mr. Ching to him."

Jean did not reply at once. Now that she had calmed down, she was not ready to give up her sleuthing. She made a counterproposal.

"How would it be if we just drive into the grounds and take a look?"

Louise agreed to this. They went back and drove between the pillars. This time no one stopped them. Louise parked the car, and the girls started to walk through a garden. The flowers were so gorgeous that for a few moments the Danas forgot why they had come to the place.

The pathway led to the rear of the house and onto a runway. Standing not far from the building was a small plane. There was a field behind the craft.

"It's the same one we saw overhead!" Louise exclaimed. "I remember those numbers on the fusilage."

"That explains why they were buzzing us," Jean said. "The people in the plane and in the house are doing something they don't want outsiders to know about."

Her sister nodded. "And I'd like to bet one of the persons is Charlie Ching."

The two young sleuths discussed whether or not they should act as if nothing were wrong and ring the bell.

"Intuition tells me not to try it," Louise said at last.

Jean was inclined to be more daring, but agreed to walk back to the car. "If we're going to call on the people, let's do it politely. We'll drive up to the front door and ask to see Mr. Ching."

"You've forgotten that we're not supposed to know where he lives," Louise reminded her.

Jean said, "I realize this." Then she grinned. "If we're asked how we know, why don't we just say we have been to Dr. Snyder's?"

"And then what? We don't want to get the poor podiatrist into trouble just because his nurse was talkative."

Jean was not ready to give up. "We might not have to say any more than that. The person who answers the door will assume that it's all right to let us in. After that, we'll have to proceed as we think best."

The thought made the girls walk toward the car

faster. They were several feet from it when they heard a dog bark angrily. A large German Shepherd was racing toward them at top speed.

Instantly the Danas began to run. Both wondered whether they could outdistance the growling animal and get into their car before he caught up to them.

Jean got ahead of her sister. Breathless, she urged, "Faster, Louise. *Faster!*"

In the nick of time, the two girls reached the car, yanked the doors open, and slid inside. Not two seconds later the dog came at them yelping. He put his front paws against the glass of Louise's window and snarled at her.

"Go home!" she ordered him. "Get down!"

He paid no attention, so she started the motor. Still he persisted, as if determined to get at the girls. Louise wondered what to do. She did not want to injure the animal, yet she did not see how she could shake him off without doing so.

Finally she decided to try backing up very slowly. The move seemed to satisfy the dog that the callers were leaving. He jumped down.

"Thank goodness," said Jean.

Louise drove all the way to the main road in reverse. The dog stood still, his eyes fixed keenly on the Danas. He did not attempt to follow.

"He's a well-trained watchdog," Jean remarked.

Her sister said nothing. She paused at the pillars and looked in both directions. No one was coming, so she backed around, then headed for Newport Beach.

"That was a narrow escape!" Jean said. Her pounding heart had quieted down.

Louise said she was more convinced than ever that they had found the man who had stolen the valuable empress's crown. "He's so well guarded, I wonder if we'll ever be able to see him."

Jean stared at her sister in surprise. "You aren't giving up, are you?" she asked.

"Oh no!" Louise replied. "But a few hours ago I felt that we had all but solved this mystery."

"I did too," Jean admitted.

When the girls reached the Starfish Motel, they hurried inside, eager to tell their Aunt Harriet what had happened.

As they passed the desk, Jean noticed a letter in their mailbox. It was addressed to both of them, and held a message, "Phone your friend Evelyn at once!"

Louise and Jean glanced at each other. Did Evelyn have good news for them, or bad?

CHAPTER XIV

The Phoenix

As soon as Louise and Jean reached their room, Louise called the hospital and spoke to Evelyn.

"Is everything all right?" she asked.

Evelyn answered, "Of course. I'm so happy. My brother is here!"

"You've seen him and talked to him?" Louise inquired.

"Yes. Oh, he looks wonderful!"

"I'm relieved," said Louise. "When Jean and I received the note telling us to call you, we were afraid there might be bad news."

Evelyn admitted she did have some disturbing information. "I received another threatening phone call from Mr. Brink. But I'm not going to worry about it any longer. Franklin will be able to take care of the whole thing, I'm sure. By the way, I made a reservation for him at your motel, so you'll be able to see him."

"That's great!" Louise said. "What time will he be here?"

Evelyn said he was going to have dinner with her in the hospital room and stay until visiting hours were over. "He plans to go to the motel after that."

At nine o'clock Franklin Starr arrived with his bags. Louise and Jean were waiting in the lobby with Aunt Harriet for the tall, dark-haired young man. They all went to his room and sat down to exchange news. Finally the conversation got around to the possible lawsuit against Evelyn.

"I'll go to see this Mr. Brink first thing tomorrow morning," Franklin promised. "I understand you girls have already been to his office. What's your impression of him?"

Jean burst out, "Not good!"

Franklin laughed. "I'm glad you warned me. What do you know about him?"

Louise said that the girls suspected him of double-dealing. "We think both he and Moss Engels, the boy who was driving, are not telling the truth. Brink wants to get as much out of this case as he can."

"I see," Franklin replied. "Now tell me what you Danas have been doing. I hear from Evelyn that you have two or three mysteries on the docket!"

Aunt Harriet spoke. "Indeed they have. My nieces have already had some harrowing experiences, trying to solve the cases." She described a few of the incidents.

Franklin looked worried. "Do you think it's worth taking such chances, just to unravel a devilish scheme?"

Louise and Jean answered together. "Yes, we do."

Between them, they brought him up-to-date on the strange disappearance of Sally Benson and Peter Wing. "We're sure they never met each other before," Louise added, "so it's not likely they went off together except under pressure."

"You mean they were forced to go by somebody else?" Franklin asked.

The Danas nodded. Louise said, "In plain terms, we think both of them have been kidnapped!"

The young man wanted to know if the girls had thought of any reason for this. Both said they had theories, but up to the present nothing more.

"We tracked down Peter Wing's parents and learned that he worked off and on at odd jobs. Maybe one of his employers was Charlie Ching.

Aunt Harriet said, "I forgot to tell you girls that after you told me the numbers on the fusilage of the plane at *Shou-Lao*, I got in touch with the authorities and learned the license had been issued to a man named Rizzo."

"Oh, Aunt Harriet, you're wonderful!" Louise exclaimed, and Jean ran across the room to hug her aunt.

Aunt Harriet chuckled and went on, "Rizzo not only owns the plane, but he's the pilot."

"And a daredevil pilot!" Jean said, and told Franklin Starr how he had buzzed the girls in their car.

Louise now explained about the stolen crown and what they had deciphered from the invitations.

"The message was signed 'Wing,' and we decided this was probably Peter Wing. Would you mind calling on Mr. Ching and Mr. Rizzo?"

Franklin laughed. "If you promise they won't set the dog on me!"

He asked where the place was. "I'll tell you what I'll do," he added. "First thing tomorrow morning I'll rent a car and visit Mr. Brink. After that, suppose I pick you girls up. You can point out the place to me, and if you don't want to enter the grounds, you can wait somewhere along the road until I come out."

He added grimly, "Also, if I don't return within a reasonable length of time, you'd better get the police and rescue me!"

He asked the girls what approach he could use in trying to speak to Mr. Ching. Louise had a suggestion. "How about telling him that you have just returned from China, and you thought Mr. Ching would be interested in the political news from that country."

"That sounds good," the young man answered. "And if he lets me inside, then what am I to do?"

Jean replied, "The main thing is to find the Phoenix. Usually they are bright red, but the one Mr. Ching has may be gold or silver. If you aren't making any progress, how about starting to admire any Asiatic art objects he may have around? If you think he's becoming suspicious, you might pretend that you thought you were talking to the other Charles Ching, the professor. He has many beautiful pieces from Asia in his home."

Franklin grinned. "I'm beginning to like my assignment," he said, his eyes twinkling. "Well, I'd better get to bed. May I sit with you at breakfast?"

"Indeed you may," Aunt Harriet replied. "We'd love to have you. Is eight o'clock too early?"

"Not for a man who's going to have a very busy day," he answered.

At about ten the following morning, after his appointment with Mr. Brink, Franklin picked up the girls in his car. Louise immediately asked him what he had learned from the lawyer.

Franklin's brow creased and he looked worried. "I couldn't get to first base with him. He pompously said his witnesses have already signed statements. I'll probably have to get a lawyer."

Louise and Jean told him of their talk with Eric Reese in the hospital. "He told us he had not seen Evelyn yank the wheel away from the driver. He's sorry he signed any paper saying he had, and will now deny it."

"You're sure you can trust him?" Franklin asked.

"Oh, absolutely. He's very nice. I got the impression that he and Moss Engels didn't see eye to eye on many things."

When Louise and Jean reached the entrance to *Shou-Lao*, the girls hopped out. Jean said, "I do hope you will see the Phoenix on the teakwood stand, Franklin. Also look for an opening in the stand."

"I'll do my best," he replied, and drove into the estate.

The girls looked for a place to hide in case anyone should go into or out of *Shou-Lao*. A few feet up the road on the opposite side were several large trees. The sisters chose two large ones.

For some time it was very quiet and no one passed along the road. But suddenly Louise and Jean became aware of a car approaching at great speed. They peered from their hiding places, and saw a large automobile whizzing by them.

With a squeal of brakes it turned into the driveway of the estate. The girls caught a glimpse of the driver.

"*Brink!*" Jean exclaimed. "Do you suppose he's after Franklin?"

Her sister replied, "I doubt it. I think Brink is just the kind of a lawyer Ching would have! But what a complication if he finds Franklin!"

Jean said she wished there were some way to

warn Franklin, but it was out of the question. The vicious dog had not appeared, and the girls thought that might be because Brink was expected.

"Oh dear," said Jean, "I wish I could eavesdrop at that house!"

In a little while Franklin Starr drove down the driveway and picked the girls up. Immediately Louise asked him if he had met Brink at the house.

"Brink?" he repeated in amazement. "No. Why did you ask?"

Jean answered. "We saw him drive in. Did you meet Ching and Rizzo?"

"Yes, but apparently they didn't want me to meet Brink."

"That was a lucky break for you!" Louise commented.

Franklin agreed and then told the girls that he had had little trouble locating the Phoenix. It was in an office beyond the living room and was perched on a teakwood stand.

"It's bright red and quite ornate. I walked all around it, admiring its beauty, and looking for any kind of an opening, I saw none. Pretending that I wanted to get the feel of such a beautiful object as the Phoenix, I picked it up and even dragged the stand behind me nonchantly. Nothing fell out."

Louise asked, "What were Ching and Rizzo like?"

"Ching was tall and had a commanding air about

him. He wore American clothes. Rizzo was short and swarthy. Both had piercing dark eyes."

When Franklin and the girls reached the Starfish Motel, Aunt Harriet was seated in the lobby. "How did you make out?" she asked.

Franklin Starr repeated his story. She was amazed, but sorry to hear that he had not discovered the stolen empress's crown.

"Do you suppose," Jean asked, "that Peter Wing's message in the invitations was untrue?"

Louise shook her head. "From what his parents told us about him, I'd be willing to guess he was telling the truth."

Jean said suddenly, "If that crown is hidden inside the teakwood stand, I'm going to find it!"

The others glanced at her. She asked, "Franklin, would you be willing to take Louise and me to Ching's house? I thought of a way we might get his attention without having the dog attack us."

"How?" Aunt Harriet asked.

"Why don't we just tell Mr. Ching and Mr. Rizzo that Peter Wing had disappeared and his parents are exceedingly worried about him. Then we might ask Ching to tell us all he knows about Wing and in this way help trace him." She grinned. "We'll look as innocent as possible."

Louise was enthusiastic about the scheme. She turned to Franklin for an answer. He said he would be glad to take the girls.

"Shall we go tomorrow morning?" Louise asked.

"Sorry, I can't," he replied.

Seeing the expression of disappointment on the faces of the two young sleuths, he added, "Let's go today, right after lunch!"

Later, when they were ready to leave, Aunt Harriet kissed the girls good-by and shook hands with Franklin Starr. "I wish all of you good luck," she said.

CHAPTER XV

The Vanished Bird

As Franklin Starr and the Dana girls were about to leave the motel, Mrs. Menken walked in. The chairman of the student culture-and-talent pageant seemed upset.

"Hello, girls," she said. "Do you have any news for me?"

"Not right now," Louise answered, "but we're on our way to try to retrieve the original crown."

"Oh, I hope you can do it!" the woman cried. She was breathing heavily, her face was red, and she blinked continuously.

Jean spoke. "Before we tell you any more, I'd like to present Mr. Franklin Starr. Franklin, this is Mrs. Menken, who is head of the pageant."

The two shook hands, and Franklin wished her luck in solving the mystery. She then asked the girls to tell her more about what they were going to do.

The woman was astonished at all they had learned and told them how grateful she was. Nevertheless, Mrs. Menken seemed sad.

"Do you realize that there are only two days left before the pageant? And I have no crown!" she wailed.

Louise tried to soothe and encourage her by saying, "You may have it by tonight!"

Mrs. Menken remarked that this was only part of the problem. "I want Sally Benson back! Do you realize that her disappearance puts a damper on the whole competition?"

The chairman said that not only were the towns-people talking and complaining that the police had not been able to find Sally, but that the other girls in the pageant were becoming nervous.

"I'm afraid the whole thing will be a poor show," Mrs. Menken said. "And I had such high hopes of something new, different, and fine."

Louise put an arm around the woman. "Instead of these negative thoughts, how about wishing us luck as we search for the crown and perhaps learn more about Sally's whereabouts?"

Mrs. Menken promised to do this. She smiled at Franklin and the girls and said, "Don't let any harm come to yourselves!"

She waved good-by. Franklin walked with Louise and Jean to his car. They rode directly to *Shou-Lao*. The dog did not appear.

Mr. Ching and Mr. Rizzo were there. They let the visitors in, but were not cordial. Neither of the men invited Franklin and the Danas to enter beyond the front hall. The pair stood quiet, waiting for the others to speak.

It was an awkward silence, but finally Franklin broke it. "I was so impressed with your Phoenix statue that I couldn't resist bringing my friends to see it. I have told them how magnificent it is—a real work of art."

Without being invited to do so, he had started into the living room toward the adjoining office, where the bird stood. Louise and Jean walked behind him. Ching and Rizzo looked annoyed, but said nothing and followed the callers.

Suddenly Franklin exclaimed, "The Phoenix is not here!"

Not only was the Phoenix gone, but the carved teakwood stand as well. In their place stood a small table with a large plant on it.

Still Ching and Rizzo said nothing. Franklin asked, "Where is the Phoenix?"

"Honorable bird has been sold," Ching replied, but said nothing more.

Franklin asked about the teakwood stand.

"That has been sold also," was the reply.

Louise and Jean were stunned. They felt downcast. The young sleuths had come so close to solving the mystery, only to be frustrated!

Franklin asked if he could take the girls to see the bird at the new owner's. Ching shook his head.

"I do not wish to give the name of the buyer," he said.

He and Rizzo started walking toward the front door, indicating that they wanted their visitors to leave.

Louise and Jean had other plans, however. They paused, and Louise said, "We understand that a young man named Peter Wing works for you. He has disappeared and his parents are frantic. Can you tell us anything about where he might be?"

Ching and Rizzo scowled, but Rizzo answered politely, "He used to do odd jobs for us now and then. He hasn't been here lately. We have no idea where he is."

Ching added, "I am truly sorry to hear that his honorable parents are worried. I hope they will find him soon."

By this time the visitors had reached the front door and Ching opened it. Louise shot a quick question at him.

"You're really a South Korean, aren't you?"

"Yes, I am."

At once Rizzo added, "But you left there and went to Taiwan when you were very young."

Ching puckered his brow as if he were not sure what Rizzo meant, but almost instantly he said, "Yes, that is correct."

Louise and Jean glanced at each other. They felt pretty sure this was not the truth.

"What does *Shou-Lao* mean?" Jean asked.

"In ancient Chinese mythology *Shou-Lao* was the God of Long Life," Ching replied politely.

On their way back to the Starfish Motel, Franklin said, "Why did you ask Mr. Ching if he is a South Korean?"

Louise answered, "Because I have had the idea that someone from South Korea wants Amalie to win the contest. With Sally Benson out of the way, this seems like a foregone conclusion."

Franklin looked surprised. "Oh?"

Louise told him the various clues in the mystery that had led her to this conclusion. He remarked, "It sounds reasonable. I think you girls are wonderful to have figured out so much."

Louise laughed. "Don't congratulate us until we solve the case!"

Presently Jean said she felt a new idea could be added to the others. "I have a hunch that the lawyer, Mr. Brink, took the Phoenix and the teakwood stand. Ching figured it would be safe with him until the storm about the bird blows over. I'm more convinced than ever that the priceless crown is hidden in that teakwood stand."

"A logical conclusion," Franklin said. "If so, then you girls have practically established that Ching is the villian behind the mystery. He's a thief, a kidnapper, and a would-be poisoner. But if he wants Amalie to win, why would he want to poison her?"

Louise agreed it was indeed a puzzle. "The problem right now is, how are we going to prove all these things against him? And how can we get Sally back and recover the real crown in time for the contest?"

CHAPTER XVI

Worthwhile Tip

AFTER reviewing all angles of the case, Louise suggested that she and Jean call on Mr. and Mrs. Wing. "If they haven't heard from their son, I think they should contact the FBI, and perhaps have *Shou-Lao* investigated."

Jean agreed, and Franklin Starr said he thought this might be a good idea. He dropped them off at the motel and told the girls he wanted to see Evelyn.

"I hope you learn something worthwhile," he said, smiling. "You two are absolutely amazing."

Louise and Jean laughed, then went to their room. They burst in on Aunt Harriet to tell her that the Phoenix and the teakwood stand were gone.

"Mr. Ching said he had sold them," Louise added. "But Jean and I think he gave them to Mr. Brink to hide."

Jean heaved a great sigh. "I was so sure we'd get the crown back that we even told Mrs. Menken we might bring it with us. She was so upset I hate to face her and tell her we failed."

Aunt Harriet patted her niece on the shoulder. "Mrs. Menken is disturbed, yes, but actually she's a very sensible and practical person. I doubt that she really expected you to retrieve it." Miss Dana changed the subject. "I have information for you."

"About the mystery?" Louise asked eagerly.

Aunt Harriet shook her head. "It's good news, though. Your friends Chris and Ken are coming here to stay for a few days."

"Great!" the sisters exclaimed.

Aunt Harriet chuckled. "They told me on the phone that they were planning to help you girls solve your mysteries."

Jean pursed her lips. "Maybe that's just what we need—the aid of two good strong young men!"

The others smiled, then Aunt Harriet reminded her nieces that they were invited to a rehearsal of the contestants.

Louise and Jean quickly combed their wind-blown hair, then went downstairs. The culture-and-talent contestants were practicing a slow promenade in evening dresses. These were not the gowns, however, that they would wear in the final performance.

"Don't they look wonderful!" Louise exclaimed.

Jean nodded. "And they walk as straight as
soldiers and with as much precision. They must
have worked a lot when we weren't around."

As Amalie passed them, she smiled at Louise and
Jean. Some of the others did also, but the Dana girls
felt that Amalie was the most gracious.

When the rehearsal was over, Louise and Jean
scooted back to their room and asked Aunt Harriet
if she would like to go with them to call on Mr. and
Mrs. Wing.

"Yes, I would. I'd enjoy meeting Peter's parents."

Fortunately the Wings were at home and greeted
Aunt Harriet with low bows. Louise gave them the
latest news after they told the callers that they had
heard nothing either from Peter or about him.

"We feel," Jean said, "that Mr. Ching and Mr.
Rizzo are at the bottom of the whole complicated
mystery. We think the authorities should investigate their home and see if they can uncover anything that would prove the men guilty."

Mrs. Wing shrank back in her chair, and her
husband looked alarmed. Finally he said, "All I
could tell the FBI would be that we suspect those
men kidnapped our son. But we have no proof."

Aunt Harriet said, "Mr. and Mrs. Benson feel
the same way you do, but we're going to talk to
them too. If both families asked the FBI to investigate at *Shou Lao*, I'm sure they will."

Mr. Wing said, "Perhaps you're right, Miss Dana. We very much want our son back, and want him back unharmed. If your theories are correct, Peter and Miss Benson won't be released until after the pageant is over. Do you think Mr. Ching and Mr. Rizzo know about the message hidden in the invitations Peter sent to you?"

Louise answered, "We're not sure, but the fact that we have been so interested in the Phoenix may have started them guessing about how we found out."

After a pause Mr. Wing said, "We will speak to the local police before we contact the FBI."

"Oh, thank you," Louise said. "Now we'll talk to Mr. and Mrs. Benson."

Mrs. Wing smiled at Louise and Jean. "I hope your theories are correct. If so, my honorable husband and I will not have to wait much longer for our son to return."

When the Danas arrived at the Starfish Motel, they found out through the house phone that Sally's parents were in their room. The girls were invited to go up.

The Bensons announced that they had received no ransom notes. The couple listened attentively to Louise and Jean's account of their call on Ching and Rizzo, with Franklin Starr.

Mr. Benson warned, "If you are on the right track, it's possible you were not harmed by those men because you had Mr. Starr with you."

The remark gave Aunt Harriet's spine a tingling sensation from top to bottom. "Don't ever go there alone," she begged her nieces.

They promised, then Louise suggested that Mr. and Mrs. Benson notify the FBI about Sally's kidnapping. "Mr. Wing is calling them too."

Mrs. Benson sighed. "I was so hoping the mystery would be solved in a hurry and Sally would be brought home to us."

Although the Dana girls were delighted when Sally's father said he would call the FBI at once, the sisters felt strongly that they themselves should not stop working on the case. Louise had another idea and said she wanted to contact the local police herself.

Aunt Harriet stayed at the motel while her nieces drove down to headquarters. They went inside and asked for the captain. The girls were shown to his office.

He smiled at them and said, "You're getting quite a reputation around here as amateur sleuths. Have you some new clues to the kidnappings to give us?"

Louise said that unfortunately they did not, but she wanted to pursue another lead.

"Captain, do you know of any South Korean in this vicinity?"

"Yes," he replied. "There are two families, the Chhih Heas, and the Yun Rhees."

"Would you mind telling us where they live?"

"On the outskirts of Newport Beach," he replied. "Apparently they are very fine people. There have never been any complaints about them."

The girls thanked the captain for his information and left headquarters. Jean wanted to know if her sister intended to find these people now.

"No," Louise replied. "I first want to ask Amalie if she knows them."

Jean remarked that they could do this after the next rehearsal for the contest. The Danas hurried off to watch the practice. The minute it was over, they sought out Amalie, and complimented the lovely girl on her performance. Then, Louise brought the conversation around to the subject of South Korea.

"Amalie, have you any relatives in the United States?" she asked.

"Yes, I do," the girl replied. "Two families. They both live near here. It was through one of them that I happened to get into this pageant."

She went on to say that she loved the Yun Rhees. "I often go there. They live just outside Newport Beach."

"And what about the other family?" Louise asked.

"I do not like the Chhih Heas. They—well, they're too narrow-minded."

"In what way?" Jean asked.

Amalie answered, "They have made money in this country, but do not praise the United States. All they talk about is the glory of South Korea!"

Louise and Jean were startled. Their hearts beat faster. Here was a possible clue!

At this moment two of the other contestants came to pick up Amalie for a special session. The Danas said good-by and went to their room. As they entered, the phone was ringing.

Jean answered it. "Hi!" she cried out. "How are you, Evelyn?"

"I'm being released from here," the girl reported. "Of course I must use a wheel chair and crutches, but I won't mind, just as long as I can be with you girls. My brother will bring me. I'll be there by suppertime."

Louise and Jean were delighted and said they were very happy for Evelyn. "We have so much to tell you," Jean said, "but we'll wait until you get here."

"I'm going to have the room right next to yours," Evelyn said. "Well, good-by for now."

As soon as the conversation ended, Louise and Jean hurried into Aunt Harriet's room and told her about Evelyn.

"That's wonderful," Miss Dana said. With a smile, she added, "I can keep her company."

"Oh, I'm sure she'd love that!" Jean exclaimed.

Aunt Harriet suggested that her nieces run down

to the beach to take a dip. "But be careful, and don't let anybody bury you in the sand again!"

The sisters laughed, and Jean said, "I think a swim will do us both good."

When the girls reached the beach, they found many people on it. Jean giggled. "We're safe now!"

The Danas ran down to the water, dived through a wave, and swam out to where a lifeguard was bouncing up and down in a boat that was moored. The girls stopped to chat with him a few seconds.

"Hi!" Jean called out to the golden-tanned young man who held a megaphone to his lips and shouted at some children, telling them to keep off the ropes. His large sunglasses and broad-brimmed hat hid his face, which soon softened into a friendly smile.

"Ah, a couple of cute mermaids have come to visit me!" he said.

The water swelled into gentle waves, easing the sisters beyond the boat. "I feel like a fish when I'm in the ocean!" Louise exclaimed, taking a long stroke.

"Don't go out any farther," the guard warned. "We've just heard there's a shark in these waters."

"Thanks," said Louise. "We don't want to meet him!"

Louise and Jean continued their swim. An hour later they returned to the motel. On the elevator hung a large sign, "Out of order."

"Then it's up the stairs for us," Jean said, starting toward them.

Just before they reached their own floor, the girls heard a familiar voice, "I'm here! I'm coming to meet you!"

"Evelyn!" Jean cried.

"Hi!" Louise called out. "Take it easy. We'll be there in a minute."

When the Danas were several steps from the top, they could see Evelyn in a wheel chair, just approaching the stairway. Suddenly they froze in disbelief. An unseen hand behind the wheel chair gave it a sudden hard push. Evelyn and the chair rolled forward down the steps!

CHAPTER XVII

Which Ching?

"Oh!" Evelyn screamed, as she fell forward, out of the wheel chair.

Louise's and Jean's reactions were instantaneous. They must save Evelyn, yet not let the wheel chair hit them! They moved over to the rail and grabbed it with their left hands.

Bracing themselves, the Danas put out their right hands and caught their friend. The impact was so strong, that Louise and Jean teetered for several seconds before regaining their balance.

The wheel chair had clattered past them, down the wide stairway. It landed on its side on the floor below.

All three girls sat down on the stairs. Louise and Jean were worried about the effect of the headlong pitch on Evelyn.

"Are you all right?" Louise asked her.

"I—I guess so," Evelyn replied. She was shaking.

"Girls, I didn't fall accidentally. Somebody pushed me!"

"I thought so," Jean replied. "Maybe I can find out who it was."

She stood up and scooted to the top of the steps. A long hallway stretched out in front of her. Nobody was in it. Had some person come from one of the rooms, then run back?

Jean went all the way down the hall. There was a door at the rear that opened onto an outside stairway. No one was there.

She heaved a sigh, thinking, "If that attacker came in this way and went out here, we may never find out who he was."

Jean returned to the other two girls and asked, "Evelyn, do you want Louise and me to carry you to your room, or shall I see if the wheel chair is in working order?"

Evelyn stood up. "I think I can hop with your assistance."

Louise and Jean helped her negotiate the steps. Then, slowly, they went to Evelyn's room. The Danas lifted her into bed and asked if she felt all right.

"Yes, I do, really." Evelyn smiled faintly. "But I admit that the bed feels good."

Jean offered to retrieve the wheel chair. In a few minutes she had dragged it up the stairs. One wheel was bent, giving the chair a strange, sideways tilt, as Jean rolled it along the corridor.

It looked so ridiculous that when she entered Evelyn's room, the girls burst into laughter. This relieved the tension under which they had all been. The Danas sat down to try figuring out who had shoved Evelyn down the stairway.

She said at once, "I'm sure it was Mr. Brink. He's mad because my brother's here and Franklin won't take any nonsense from him."

Louise had another idea. "I think you're right that he has something to do with it. But I doubt that he would have caused this accident, for fear of being caught."

Jean asked her, "Have you anybody else in mind?"

Louise thought a moment, then said, "I wonder if Moss Engels has left the hospital and is well again."

"Let's find out," Jean suggested, and went to the phone. After a conversation with the office at the hospital, she reported to the other girls that both Moss Engels and Eric Reese had been discharged the previous day.

"I'd hate to accuse him of such a thing," Evelyn remarked. "When I met him just before taking the trip in the car, he didn't seem like a bad sort. He was kind of a braggart. I'm inclined to think maybe this whole business of blaming me was Brink's idea, not Moss's.

The conversation was interrupted by the ringing

of the telephone in the next room. Louise dashed out into the hall and her own bedroom. The call was from Professor Ching. He seemed excited.

"Louise," he said, "could you and Jean come here right away? I had a telephone message that I'm sure concerns your mystery. The person is going to call back in an hour."

"We'll drive over at once," Louise promised. She hurried to the other two girls and repeated the message. "Evie, will you be all right? I'll ask Aunt Harriet to come in. She said she wanted to keep you company."

"That's very sweet of her. Actually I think I could go to sleep. But tell her I'm here anyway."

In a short while the Dana girls were on their way to Professor Ching's home. "I wonder what the mysterious phone message was," Jean murmured.

Louise shrugged and from then on the girls were silent until they reached the house. Both were thinking up, then promptly discarding, a lot of guesses about who had contacted the professor.

He met the girls at the front door. "I'm so glad you came. My honorable wife and I have been upset over this strange call. Come in and we'll all sit down."

The girls spoke to Mrs. Ching, then seated themselves near the professor.

"A man with a deep voice telephoned me," he started to explain. "The man said, 'This is the captain. Mr. Ching's orders are being carried out.' The person gave me no chance to interrupt because he hung up."

The professor added that the "captain" had said he would telephone again in an hour with more details. "I thought if you girls listened in, you might pick up some good clue. Obviously the call is not for me, but for the Mr. Ching you told me about."

Louise said she surmised that the "captain" did not have Mr. Ching's unlisted phone number and had contacted the professor by mistake. "But this may be a very good mistake. Thank you so much, professor, for asking us to come here."

The kindly man said it was probably useless to speculate until after the second message. "In the meantime, I will tell you another story of my native country. This is a myth about a man and his wife who lived up on the Milky Way in the sky. It was called the Celestial River.

"They were very happy but did something that displeased the God of Heaven. For punishment he made the couple separate and live on opposite sides of the river. They could visit each other only on the seventh day of every seventh month. The man was called Cowherd and his wife was Heavenly Weaver-Girl. Birds formed a bridge for the wife to cross, but if it rained, the birds flew away, and she had to wait another seven years to see her husband."

"What a sad story!" Louise remarked.

Jean added, "I'm glad it's only a myth."

A clock chimed. There were still fifteen minutes before the mysterious stranger was to telephone again.

The professor said, "I'm sure you girls have heard about the Great Wall of China. But have you ever read the facts and measurements?"

"No, we haven't," they answered.

He went on, "Of course the wall was built for protection. It was started during the reign of the first united China under Emperor Shih Huang Ti in two hundred twenty-one B.C."

"Is any of the Great Wall still standing?" Louise asked.

"Oh, yes," the professor replied, "but, of course, China has expanded far beyond the wall. We estimate that at least ten thousand laborers were involved and that it took eighteen years to build."

Jean said, "It must be one of the biggest public projects of all time. How large was the wall?"

"Ten meters high, and thirty-six meters wide." Jean quickly figured it to be almost forty feet high and nearly a quarter of a mile wide.

Louise asked how long the wall had been originally, and if it was circular.

Professor Ching told the girls that it was ten thousand miles long and that it covered rugged terrain. "The wall is somewhat like a giant oval."

At this moment the telephone rang. The professor nodded, indicating that the girls were to follow him as he answered it.

The stranger, again referring to himself as the captain, said curtly, "I left Wing and the girl adrift at four and a half kilometers." He chuckled in a deep voice. "They have no power, no lights, no food, or water." The man hung up abruptly.

Professor Ching and the Danas stood in disbelief. The stranded couple was nearly three miles from shore!

The phone rang again. The girls held their breaths, but the caller was Aunt Harriet.

"Louise and Jean," she said, "Chris and Ken have arrived."

"Tell them we'll come right back to the motel," Jean said. She turned to Professor Ching. "Our friends are experts at running power boats. Louise, let's hire one and hunt for Sally and Wing!"

"Good idea," Louise agreed. She said to Professor Ching, "Would you please notify the Coast Guard immediately of the message you received?"

He promised to do so, then the girls said good-by to him and Mrs. Ching. The couple wished them luck.

"I'm afraid we'll need it," Louise said as the girls left the house.

When they reached the Starfish Motel, Ken Scott and Chris Barton were outside, waiting for them. Ken was tall, slender, blond, and good looking. Chris was dark-haired and full of fun. He started to tease the sisters about not being there when they arrived, but the girls were too worried to respond with a joke.

"We've just heard some dreadful news," Louise told them. "Let's go inside and we'll tell you and Aunt Harriet about it. We're going to need your help."

"Anything you say," Ken replied.

Miss Dana was in the lobby. When she learned what had happened to Sally Benson and Peter Wing, she was aghast. "I suppose we'll have to tell Mr. and Mrs. Benson right away. They'll want to join the search."

Jean telephoned the couple's room. There was no answer. She asked the man at the desk to page the Bensons over the loudspeaker, but still there was no reply.

"We can't wait for them any longer," Louise said. "Aunt Harriet, do we have your permission to rent a motorboat and go out to hunt for Sally and Peter?"

Miss Dana looked startled, but gave her consent. "Oh, I do hope you find them," she said. "But be careful."

The four young people changed their clothes and put on swimsuits under their slacks, shirts, and sweaters. They drove quickly to the dock, where motorboats could be rented.

While the boys were attending to this, Louise

and Jean rushed to a nearby luncheonette. They purchased several sandwiches as well as bottles of soda, enough for themselves and the stranded couple.

"We ought to have a hot drink for Sally and Wing," Louise remarked. She asked the counterman if this could be arranged. They might not use it for hours.

He was very obliging. "I'll lend you a Thermos of hot chocolate," he said, and fixed it for them.

By the time the girls returned, Ken and Chris had obtained a speedy cabin cruiser with an inboard motor.

"It's nifty," Jean said, climbing in.

Chris went straight out four and a half kilometers, then the group discussed which way they should go. For several minutes each was silent, trying to figure out a logical answer.

"We have eight choices," Chris said to himself. He listed them. "North, south, east, west, northeast, northwest, southeast, or southwest."

At the same time Ken was also considering possibilities. "If we had four boats, we could scan every inch of water," he thought. "But unfortunately, we've only got one!"

Louise and Jean were temporarily stumped, too. "We can't risk going in a wrong direction," each girl concluded. The young people all spoke again at exactly the same moment, and their conclusion was unanimous.

Louise repeated their thought. "If Sally and Peter had no power, their boat would drift. Let's take the direction in which they would drift, but turn on the motor and go a little faster so we can overtake them."

The boys studied the current, which seemed to be running southwesterly. No one talked. They all sat, grim and worried about the fate of the two kidnap victims. Could the Danas and their friends find them in time to save their lives?

CHAPTER XVIII

Daring Rescue

WHEN Chris reached four and a half kilometers from shore, he told the others, then said, "Are we ready to drift?"

His companions nodded. Chris shut off the motor, and the boat moved slowly in a southwesterly direction. He now turned on the motor. They barely crawled along. There was no conversation for several minutes, then Ken asked, "Louise and Jean, are you sure that your villain Mr. Ching wasn't playing a trick on you?"

"What kind of trick? And why should he do that?" Jean asked.

"To get you girls out of the way. He probably figured you were nearing the truth and thought it was high time to send you on some kind of an errand."

Louise had a different theory. "Maybe Ching was going to pull some trick while we Danas were out of the way. But I believe that by kidnapping Sally he has played the worst trick of all. What more can he do?"

"Kidnap you girls also," Ken replied. Then he smiled. "It's a good thing we showed up here when we did."

Jean hastened to say, "I guess so. Anyway, let's not argue about it while we're tossing in this rough ocean."

In a few minutes Louise looked up at the sky and scowled. "If I'm not mistaken, a thunderstorm's coming up."

The others agreed and Chris said, "We're right in its path. Do you think we should go back?"

"No!" the Danas said together, and Louise added. "The storm won't hurt us. We can crawl into the cabin. We must find Sally and Wing. Their drifting boat will be at the mercy of the storm."

Jean said, "Chris, would it be possible for you to follow the path of the ocean's current at a faster pace?"

"I think so," he replied, accelerating the motor.

He also flicked on the radio. They were just in time to hear a broadcast storm warning. The announcer also said that the Coast Guard was looking for a couple lost on the ocean.

When the man finished, Ken said, "He didn't mention the names of the people they're after. Do you think he meant Sally and Wing?"

"I'm sure he did," Louise replied. "But they don't want to alert the men who set them adrift, and give those villians any idea the couple will be found."

Jean had gone into the cabin and now began pulling out drawers, looking for binoculars. She found two pairs and brought them outside. "I don't know whether it's too dark for these to help, but let's try them." She handed one pair to her sister and used the others herself.

The Danas gazed in all directions but saw nothing. The sky looked weird. Behind the girls, the sun was shining, but ahead it was pitch-black.

The cruiser cut through the water, which was becoming more choppy every minute. The rain had started to fall, and the wind was strong. The four searchers huddled in the cabin.

A few minutes later there was a brilliant flash of lightning. Louise, who was still looking through the binoculars, cried out, "I see a boat! And it's not a Coast Guard cutter, because the boat has no cabin. Maybe Sally and Wing are inside!"

"Where did you see it?" Chris asked.

Louise pointed east, and Chris turned his craft accordingly. They bounced and rolled and water sprayed over the cruiser.

Louise and Jean had brought their own searchlights and now beamed them ahead. Soon they were near enough to look inside the other boat.

"It's empty!" Jean exclaimed. "Oh, this means

that if Sally and Wing were in it, they were washed overboard!"

"What shall I do now?" Chris asked.

Louise heaved a desolate sigh. "I guess all we can do is look in the vicinity."

Chris aimed his craft in a wide circle around the abandoned boat. The storm had abated a little. It was still very dark so the searchlights were used continuously.

"Let's yell their names," Chris suggested. He started and the others joined in.

"Sally! Sal-ly! Wing! Wi-i-ing!"

There was no response, only the sound of the wind and the buffeting waves. Chris continued to steer in ever-widening circles.

"Let's call out again," Louise urged.

The group tried it at ten-second intervals for nearly five minutes. Everyone was straining his eyes, and the two searchlights were playing over the water.

"Oh, look!" Chris exclaimed. "There's somebody's arm sticking out of the water!"

The others concentrated on it, and the Danas used their binoculars. "It's a man's arm!" Louise shouted. "Head that way!"

"If I get any closer, we might hit the person and injure him," Chris said.

"But we must rescue the poor fellow somehow!" Jean announced. "Shall we throw out a life preserver?"

"He's probably too weak to use it," Ken replied. "Suppose I try swimming to him?"

"Wait a minute!" Louise said. "Why don't the three of us do it?"

"You mean all of us rescue him?"

Louise shook her head. "I mean, let's make a human chain. That will be safer in this water."

The others agreed and took off their outer clothing. In their swimsuits, Ken, being the strongest, offered to hold onto the gunwale of the cruiser. Louise would take his free hand, while Jean grabbed her sister's. The three were soon in the water, heaving up and down with the waves.

Chris tried to keep the cruiser steady. The rescuers urged the man to swim toward them. They came very near the man, who managed to swim a few strokes and reach Jean's outstretched hand.

His first words were, "Get Sally!"

Quickly he pulled himself along the human chain, murmuring all the while, "Get Sally! Get Sally! I'm Wing."

Chris helped him into the boat. He was exhausted and flopped to the deck. Chris carried him into the cabin and threw a blanket over him.

Then he grabbed the wheel, and yelled out, "Wing, where's Sally?"

"We got separated after being washed overboard," said the young man, who was of Asiatic origin.

Chris called out to the three swimmers, "Wing

"Sally! Wing!" the searchers cried out.

and Sally lost each other. He doesn't know where she is."

Louise and Jean groaned, but Jean insisted, "We must keep on trying to find her!"

By now the ocean had calmed somewhat, so the three swimmers climbed back into the cruiser.

Chris decided to take smaller circles near the drifting boat, then proceed in a widening path.

Ken said to Chris, "If Sally is still alive, she must see our searchlights. If she's just about exhausted, she might be floating."

After that no one spoke, but all kept their eyes trained attentively on the water around them.

Just as Chris had completed the second large circle, Jean cried out, "I see another arm raised!"

She pointed, and Chris headed his craft toward the area. Less than a minute later, they all saw a girl floating in the water.

"She's alive!" Louise thought.

"Sally!" Jean cried out.

The human chain slid into the water once more and Chris brought the cruiser nearer. Jean grabbed Sally's hand. The kidnapped girl was too weak to talk or even to smile her thanks. Each of the other swimmers helped her along the human chain until they reached the cruiser.

Chris jumped up from the pilot's seat and hauled her aboard. He carried the stricken girl into the cabin and laid her down. She just looked at him, still unable to speak. He put a blanket over the shivering form, then went on deck.

By this time Jean had swum back to the cruiser along the human chain, and was pulled up. Louise came next, and finally Ken, who was able to climb over by himself.

Louise and Jean were cold and weary from the nervous strain. But they instantly ducked into the cabin to see what they could do for Sally and Wing. Louise poured out the hot chocolate for the two, and almost immediately after drinking it, both fell asleep.

The Danas whispered to Chris and Ken, and it was decided that they should get the two victims to shore as quickly as possible.

By this time the sun had brightened the sky enough so they could see a good distance ahead. A gentle wind drifted over the water, causing small waves to ripple before building into larger ones. The boat rocked over them with ease as Jean and Louise gazed at their new passengers. For several minutes they lay perfectly still. Then Sally became restless, turning from one side to the other. She cried quietly. Was she having a bad dream? Should they wake her? the Danas wondered. As if answering their deep concern, the girl stopped tossing and settled into a peaceful sleep once more.

Finally Chris, using a marine chart, figured out which direction he should take.

"We're a long way from Newport Beach," he said.

A discussion followed about whether they should return there or try to reach some spot on-shore that was closer.

"We'd better pick the closest place where Sally and Wing can get medical treatment," Louise advised.

Chris looked at a nautical directory he found in the locker. After consulting it, he frowned.

"What's the matter?" Ken asked.

"There's no place this side of Newport Beach," Chris replied, "where we could safely put in."

"Then let's speed toward our place," Louise urged.

"Okay," their pilot replied.

Instead of turning toward shore, he headed north at top speed. The bow of the cabin cruiser lifted out of the water and slapped across the waves. The girls brought out the sandwiches and soda and the four ate their long overdue supper. About an hour later, they were opposite Newport Beach inlet and Chris steered the craft into the little bay.

"We're here!" Louise exclaimed. "Thank goodness!"

At that moment Sally and Wing woke. They sat up and stared at their rescuers.

"Don't try to talk," Louise advised. "But I'd like to find out how long you were in the water."

"I don't know," Sally replied. "It seemed like ages. Oh, forgive me, Peter. These are my friends, Louise and Jean Dana."

The sisters introduced Chris and Ken. After that there was an awkward pause.

Then Jean, looking straight at Wing, asked, "I want to know why you kidnapped Sally from the motel!"

CHAPTER XIX

A Disastrous Search

At Jean's question, Peter Wing looked frightened. "Is that what people are saying?" he asked.

Before the Danas could reply, Sally spoke. "It isn't true! Oh, it isn't true! I thought so at first, but then when those horrible men set us adrift, I knew Peter had nothing to do with the kidnapping."

The Danas were completely puzzled. Louise said to Sally, "We found Wing's note that you hid among the flowers."

"That was fortunate. But how did you know enough to come out on the ocean for us?" Sally asked.

Jean told them about the message Professor Ching had received. "We figured the caller didn't have Mr. Ching's unlisted number, so he phoned the professor by mistake."

"Thank goodness for that," Sally murmured.

By this time they had reached the dock. Chris

said the others should go to the motel at once. He
would return the cruiser and the Thermos, then
get a ride with someone.

"But the police!" Peter Wing cried out. "I don't
want to be arrested! I haven't done anything."

He insisted he would get a cab and immediately
go to his own home.

"Oh, please come with us," Louise urged. "We
must know the end of your story. Jean and I have
been to your house and met your parents. We'll
phone and ask them to drive right over, and get
hold of Sally's parents, too. Then everyone can
hear what happened."

Wing reluctantly agreed to go, but thought he
and Sally should be hidden until Ching and Rizzo
could be arrested. The two, with blankets over
their heads, climbed into the rear seat of the Danas'
car and squatted on the floor.

"Now no one will see us," Sally said. "But what
are we going to do when we get to the motel?"

Jean said she knew where there was a rear entrance, and they could drive directly there. The
two could scoot inside and go up to Louise and
Jean's room without being seen.

This was accomplished with no trouble. Aunt
Harriet was there and insisted that Wing use her
room and shower.

"Run the water as hot as you can stand it," she
advised.

He was embarrassed, but her kindly, motherly

approach convinced him. Aunt Harriet had brought a traveling iron with her, and while Peter was taking his shower and getting thoroughly warm, she pressed his clothes.

When he reappeared, she declared, "You look like a new person."

In the meantime, Louise had learned that Mr. and Mrs. Benson were in their own two-room suite. They hurried up at once to get Sally. Mrs. Benson alternately laughed and cried with happiness.

Mr. Benson kept staring at his daughter and saying, "Thank goodness you're safe. We can never do enough to repay the Danas for risking their lives to rescue you."

The sisters brushed the compliment aside. Then Mr. Benson said, "I'll phone the local police and ask them to call off the Coast Guard search. I'll also get in touch with the FBI and request that they have Ching and Rizzo arrested."

Still wearing the blanket, Sally went with her parents to their own quarters, but promised to return.

As soon as Wing was ready, he and Aunt Harriet appeared at Louise and Jean's door. Minutes later his parents arrived and joined them.

They bowed to the Danas. The smiling Mr. Wing said, "We do not know how to express our gratefulness to you fine young people."

Dainty Mrs. Wing added, "The heart of this

mother wishes blessings on you for saving the life of our honorable son."

The Danas smiled, then went into Aunt Harriet's room for a little while to give the Wing family a chance to have a private reunion. Chris and Ken joined the girls.

Presently Peter called the Danas and their friends in and said he would tell them all about the kidnapping.

"As you know, I worked off and on for Mr. Ching and Mr. Rizzo. For a while I did not know they were evil men. Then I began to suspect that they were thieves. Among the things they had stolen was the very beautiful, ancient empress's crown.

"One day, when they didn't know I heard them, they mentioned that a porter at this motel had told them that two girls named Dana were to be asked to become judges for the pageant. The man, Haley, later gave Ching reports, so he knew when you were coming to stay at the Starfish. Ching had learned in the meantime that you were very good amateur detectives and decided to keep an eye on you.

"I didn't know what to do," Wing went on. "I was sure that if I told my parents they would not let me work there any more. I had become very interested in what the men were doing, and I must confess I took every opportunity to pick up clues."

"You certainly did a wonderful job," Louise said, smiling. "Please go on."

Peter revealed that after the invitations for the contest were addressed, he went on an errand for a printer to Mrs. Menken's home. She was not there, but another woman had let him in and taken the package he was to deliver.

" 'What are these?' she asked me. When I said I didn't know, she opened the package. 'More invitations!' she exclaimed. 'We don't need them!'

"I don't know what made me ask her, but I said, 'May I have a few as souvenirs?' When she said yes, I helped myself to a handful. After that I got the idea of sending a secret message to you Dana girls. No doubt it was foolish of me, but I wanted to see how you might work. So I held off notifying the police about the empress's crown.

"Then, one day I overheard Ching and Rizzo plotting to kidnap Sally until the contest was over. I never did find out the reason, but I thought I should warn her right away. I was pretty sure she or her parents would notify the police."

As the young Asiatic paused, Jean said, "And then what happened?"

"Sally came to my car as I had asked her to do. She sat in the front seat next to me. Without warning, Ching and Rizzo rushed up to us and waved something sweet in front of our noses. The next thing we both knew, we woke up on the third floor of the house at *Shou-Lao*. Our hands were tied behind our backs and our ankles had strong cord around them. We also were gagged."

"How dreadful!" Aunt Harriet said. "That was wicked! Were you able to get loose?"

"No. One or the other of the two men brought us food. As soon as we finished eating, they gagged us again. Once a day they untied our ropes, one person at a time, of course, and allowed us to walk around and stretch for about twenty minutes. Then the other one got a turn. So neither of us had a chance to get away. Ching was apologetic about kidnapping me, but said he had to when they found Sally with me, and heard me warn her. They had not intended to take her until that evening, but decided to act at once.

"After you Dana girls called at the house, the men became scared you might ask the police to come and hunt for us, so they decided to take us away. We had no idea that they planned to set us adrift on the ocean, with no food, water, or lights. We were helpless and both Sally and I thought this would be the end. Sally told me about hiding the note, and we prayed that you Dana girls would find it and somehow rescue us."

Everyone in the room had sat spellbound. The story seemed unbelievable.

The Danas now told Peter Wing of the missing Phoenix and the teakwood stand on which it stood.

"You have no idea where it is?" Peter inquired.

Louise admitted that the two girls often worked on hunches. She said, "If the police don't find it anywhere in *Shou-Lao*, then we're going to investigate another place where we think it might be. We'll let you know if we have any luck."

The Danas' phone rang. Sally was on the wire, saying that Mrs. Menken and all the contestants were coming to her room to see her. They were to be sworn not to reveal that Sally was back at the motel. She would then rest for a few hours.

After that her roommate, Judy Irish, would brief Sally on all she had missed. She would be given a chance to practice the songs she planned to sing in the talent competition.

Ken, Chris, and Peter, as well as the parents, stayed with Aunt Harriet, while Louise and Jean hurried to Sally's room. The group promised to keep the secret of Sally's return and were told they would be given the full story later on.

When the contestants heard that the Dana girls were responsible for finding Sally, they cheered. Among the most enthusiastic was Amalie.

Louise thought, "If there's anything to my theory that Ching, a South Korean, engineered Sally's abduction so that Amalie, a fellow countryman, could surely win the contest, it's certain that the girl herself knows nothing about it."

Later that day Mr. Benson came to Louise and

Jean's room. He reported that the police had arrested Ching and Rizzo.

"Hooray!" Jean cried out.

"But," Mr. Benson went on, "though the authorities searched the house thoroughly they did not find the crown, the Phoenix, or the teakwood stand."

Louise asked, "And the men confessed nothing about the crown?"

Mr. Benson shook his head. "They insist they are innocent of any wrongdoing. They did, however, express their great hatred for the Danas and Peter Wing."

To avoid publicity, Louise and Jean had supper in their room. Evelyn, who felt much better physically and immeasurably relieved that the girls were back safe, joined them. She said Franklin had had to leave because of out-of-town business but would return to take her home.

While they were eating, Mrs. Menken telephoned. "I'm extremely indebted to you and the boys for what you've done, but I'm sorry the crown has not been located. I'm beside myself with worry about it, because I have no substitute to use at the pageant."

Louise said, "We still have time for one more try. I have a strong hunch about where it may be hidden."

Mrs. Menken pleaded, "Please don't fail me!"

After she had hung up, Jean said, "What's your idea, sis?"

Louise replied, "Jean, do you suppose Ching and Rizzo were working for the Chhih Heas?"

Jean was surprised. "You mean those South Korean people Amalie dislikes? The ones she said have an exaggerated sense of patriotism? And you think they might want Amalie to win the contest so badly, and were sure she would if Sally was absent, that they would resort to most anything to gain their ends?"

"I'm afraid I do," Louise replied. She looked at her wristwatch. "It's getting dark. Let's leave and head for the Chhih Heas' to see what we can find out." She got in touch with Ken and Chris, who readily agreed to accompany the girls. The four got into the Danas' car and drove off.

As they neared the large home, Ken said, "Don't you think it might be better for you girls to go in alone? They'll be less suspicious. We'll stay out here and keep watch."

"I guess you're right," Jean agreed.

The boys let Louise and Jean off in front of the house, then drove to the street corner, where they would park and walk back.

Louise rang the bell, and the door was opened by Mr. Hea. His wife stood behind him.

"Good evening," said Louise, smiling. "We're friends of Amalie's. May we come in and talk to you?"

The door was opened wider and the girls stepped into the hall. They were not asked to go any farther, but had no intention of giving up so easily.

Jean asked, "You're coming to the pageant, aren't you?"

"Of course," Mr. Hea replied. He said no more, and the sisters wondered how to proceed. They were determined to investigate the rooms that opened off the center hall.

Louise suddenly exclaimed, "Oh, what a gorgeous picture!"

She hurried into the living room to look at the Asiatic landscape hanging over the fireplace. Jean had followed her and glanced around quickly.

In one corner of the room stood the Phoenix on the carved teakwood stand!

"Oh, how perfectly fabulous!" she cried out, hurrying over to gaze at the beautiful statue of a bright-red bird.

Louise had turned and now admired it also. "Is this a Phoenix?" she asked.

"I believe so," Mr. Hea answered stiffly. Still his wife said nothing, and the two watched the Danas closely.

The Phoenix stood a little distance from the wall, so the girls could walk around it. Louise trailed one hand along the woodwork of the teakwood stand. Suddenly she found a crack with a slight indentation. She pressed it with her thumb. A door sprang open.

Jean had stopped and now both girls looked inside the cabinet. There stood the empress's exquisite stolen crown!

The next instant the girls smelled something sweet. Suddenly they became very dizzy. They swayed, holding onto each other for support, but this did no good. Together they toppled to the floor, unconscious!

CHAPTER XX

Just in Time

WHEN Louise and Jean revived, almost at the same moment, they were lying unconscious in the Chhih Heas' living room. Ken was standing beside Louise, staring down at her, a look of concern on his face. Chris was watching Jean.

The two girls opened their eyes, and the boys heaved sighs of relief. "Thank goodness you're all right!" Ken murmured.

Louise and Jean sat up. Both felt a little dizzy, and the boys suggested they not move. Finally the Danas' heads cleared completely, and Louise murmured, "How did you get here, and where are the Chhih Heas?"

The boys sat down to explain. Ken said, "When we got to the corner, we were both uneasy about what might happen to you. Two policemen were driving by in a squad car and we hailed them. We asked if they would walk with us to the house and told them you girls were attempting to solve a mystery, but that we were worried about you."

Chris said the officers had left their car and walked a few feet behind the boys. "I guess they figured if we weren't telling the truth, they didn't want to take a chance on our trying any funny business with them." Chris grinned.

"We all stepped quietly up the front porch and looked into the living-room window. We were just in time to see you two slump to the floor. We didn't know what had happened. Then Chhih Hea reached into the cabinet and pulled out the empress's crown. The woman grabbed the phoenix."

Ken went on, "That made the officers' eyes pop, and instantly one of them said, 'That couple will probably try to escape. Suppose one of you boys comes with me to guard the back door. The other two stay here!'"

Between them, Ken and Chris told how the couple had grabbed a purse and taken some money from a desk drawer. Then they had fled out the kitchen door, and straight into the arms of the waiting policeman and Ken.

"The other officer and I," Chris continued, "ran around to the rear to help. There was no chance of the Heas getting away from the four of us."

Ken said he had told the officers he wanted to check on the unconscious girls. The policeman pulled a short-wave radio out of a pocket and called headquarters for more help. "It arrived in about three minutes. Mr. Hea was made to unlock the rear door and let us in. The police took the couple away," he concluded. "But before that, the Heas confessed to their part in the mystery."

After he arrived in this country, Charlie Ching hid the crown and did not declare it to customs inspectors. He then had a cheap crown made to look like the original and mailed it to Mrs. Menken. Later he learned from a porter named Haley that the Dana girls were to be asked to act as judges, and that they were detectives. Surely the sisters would solve the mystery of the crown! To avoid its being examined too closely, Ching had sneaked into Mrs. Menken's home and sprinkled poisonous powder on the fake piece. He intended to remove the powder before the coronation.

"In the meantime Ching went to see the Chhih Heas, whom he knew, and learned that they had secretly engineered having the beautiful and innocent Amalie enter the contest. They were determined to have her win 'for the glory of South Korea,' but had misgivings when they came to the motel and saw Sally and heard her sing.

"They asked Ching to help them out. He agreed and hired the unscrupulous porter Haley at the motel to work for him. He got a friend to accompany him and disguised himself and the two men tried to force Sally out of the Danas' car, unsuccessfully. When Franklin Starr began to help Louise and Jean, they decided to distract him. The porter found an opportunity to push Evelyn and the wheel chair down the stairs."

"Did you find out who the 'captain' was?" Jean asked.

"Yes, a crooked ex-sea-captain, who would do anything for money. Ching hired him, but the man forgot the unlisted phone number Ching gave him. He has been caught, too."

"How about our car being stolen? Who did that?" Louise inquired.

"The porter. He got the phoney license plates from Ching."

As the story was finished, Jean burst out, "Oh, you boys are marvelous! This means the whole mystery has been solved!"

Louise reminded her, "All but one part of it. Who will wear the crown? Jean, how do you feel? Not woozy any more? Will you be able to stop at Mrs. Menken's and tell her?"

"Oh yes," Jean answered.

Chris laughed. "I guess you can't keep a good detective down."

Ken brought their car to the front door, then the others climbed in and set off to Mrs. Menken's home. When she was told the good news, she cried out, "This is incredible! Oh, you wonderful, wonderful people! You mean the crown is really mine again?"

"We certainly do," Louise replied. "The police took your beautiful empress's crown for safekeeping until you claim it. Also, I guess you'll have to prefer charges against the Chhih Heas for hiding stolen property."

When the girls arrived at the motel with Ken and Chris, they were met by an excited Evelyn Starr and her brother Franklin. He had obtained a confession from Moss Engels, who had retracted his story completely. The young man admitted that Evelyn was in no way responsible for the automobile accident and he took the full blame.

"It wasn't easy for him to do," Franklin said. "Moss told me he was afraid he'd lose his license and his car. He met Brink when the lawyer was calling on a client in the hospital and had encouraged Moss to let him handle the case, probably because Moss's family is wealthy. He had promised the boy full immunity. To be sure Moss wouldn't change his mind," Franklin went on, "I got him to write his confession."

From a pocket he pulled out a letter addressed "To Whom It May Concern." The inside sheet gave full details of the accident, and Moss had signed it.

"Oh, Evelyn, I'm so happy for you!" Louise exclaimed. "And now let me tell you our story."

When Louise told her about the girls' experience two hours earlier, Evelyn was aghast. "Those wicked people!" she cried out. "They might have killed you!"

Louise said she did not think the Chhih Heas would have gone that far. The most they had hoped to do was get away with the very valuable empress's crown.

"Speaking of the crown," said Franklin, "when is the pageant?"

"Tomorrow," Louise told him.

"That doesn't give Sally much time for training or interviews," he said.

Evelyn told the others that she had watched Sally practice all afternoon. "She was great. Several judges were watching her and each had an interview with her." Evelyn smiled. "I suppose you Danas don't have to question her. You know her pretty well by this time."

Louise and Jean beamed, then the older girl said, "I have been wondering about something. Do you think anyone will feel that Jean and I are prejudiced in our voting because of all that has happened?"

"No, I don't think so," Evelyn replied. "You've proved your integrity. Anyway, it would be too late to get replacements."

Jean said that her sister had a point. "I'm going to call Mrs. Menken and ask her if she thinks we should resign." The young detective went to the phone and had a long conversation with the chairman. She came back smiling. "Everything's all right," Jean reported.

The following morning the Danas were told that the girls in the pageant were to practice part of the day at Memorial Hall next to the armory. The contestants were not to see or talk to anyone outside their group except in an emergency.

Evelyn giggled. "I guess they're getting some secret instructions. After all, they haven't even been in Memorial Hall until now."

All day long the motel buzzed with excitement in anticipation of the evening's performance. By seven o'clock the ticket holders were ready for the short walk to the pageant.

When the Danas' group arrived they were amazed at the scene. The main room of the hall had become a garden! Garlands of flowers festooned the walls.

From the stage at the far end, a runway had been built that extended halfway across the room. A pagoda had been set up at the rear of the stage. It was decorated with greenery and wisteria, giving the set the appearance of an Asiatic garden.

"It's beautiful!" said Aunt Harriet to her nieces. "By the way, I'm sitting with Evelyn, Franklin, the Bensons, and the Wings tonight. You girls will be up front with the other judges, I assume."

"That's right," Jean answered.

By eight o'clock, Memorial Hall was filled with people, and the orchestra was playing a medley of catchy tunes. The judges took their places. They were evenly divided between teen-agers and older men and women.

Now curtains at the rear of the garden opened, and a man stepped out. Loud applause greeted him as he walked to the front of the stage.

"Who is he?" Aunt Harriet asked Mrs. Benson.

The woman did not know, so the question was passed on to Evelyn. She whispered back, "He's Hal Hunter, one of the teen-agers' favorite singers."

After greeting the audience, he said, "I have been asked to tell you that everyone of the contestants deserves a crown. Each has worked hard to put on a good show for you. We'll start with a song."

As the audience clapped, the curtains were drawn back all the way. Twenty attractive young women stood there, smiling.

Hal now began "In an Asiatic Garden," and the girls joined in the chorus. It was a sentimental, happy tune, which the onlookers loved.

When the piece was finished, the contestants sat on chairs that had been assigned to them. Hal introduced Mrs. Menken, who came forward, extended a welcome to everyone there, then said she had an unusual story to tell. She gave the history of the crown, which would be placed on the head of the winner, making her empress for the year.

"Our theme is Asiatic," she said, "and our judges are being asked to appraise the contestants mainly from that angle. This is not easy, and I can tell you that the girls onstage have done a magnificent job."

She now told how old the empress's crown was, and that as soon as this show was over, it would be presented to a museum.

"I'm certainly glad of that," Aunt Harriet murmured to Mrs. Benson, who was next to her. "It's too valuable to be in someone's home, where it can easily be stolen."

As Mrs. Menken finished, the audience responded with plaudits and cheers. The magnificent crown was wheeled out on a stand and placed in the aisle that separated the contestants into two groups. There were oh's and ah's from the audience.

Hal Hunter, as master of ceremonies, stepped forward and explained that after much thought the judges had chosen ten of the contestants to appear in the finals.

"When they have displayed their talents, five finalists will be announced," he added. "From these, four runners-up and the empress will be chosen."

While the judges were making their decisions,

there were a ballet number and guitar solo. Then Hal said he was ready to announce the five finalists. Utter silence filled the hall as the listeners waited tensely.

Among the group, to the delight of Aunt Harriet and the Bensons, were Sally, her roommate Judy, and Amalie. They did not know the other two.

These five were to sit in the front on one side. Again, there was thunderous applause as the five came forward and sat down.

All were smiling happily. Each realized what an honor it was, whether or not she were to be chosen as the empress.

Hal said, "I have not mentioned the costumes these young ladies are wearing. I urge you to take special note. Each girl made her own and planned her individual style."

Everyone had to admit that each gown was truly Asiatic in style. Sally, with her blond hair, looked lovely in a soft lavender satin that had been wound around her slim body from neck to ankles. Pale yellow flowers had been painted on the satin. The gown had long sleeves, which rippled from shoulder to wrist. Her slippers matched perfectly.

The five contestants were given questions to answer. All the replies were extemporaneous, but the girls did remarkably well. After each one, the onlookers clapped enthusiastically.

Now it was time for the final talent show. While Amalie played a brilliant, original piano solo, Judy changed into a swimsuit made of Asiatic silk and did a perfect Chinese acrobatic act.

Next Sally was asked to sing. Her Chinese lullabies were enthusiastically applauded. The final two girls each performed well, then Hal announced that there would be a short intermission, allowing time for the judges to make their final selections.

While waiting, Miss Dana recalled how after solving each mystery, her nieces always longed for another. Aunt Harriet wondered what the next one might be, but did not find out until later, when *The Hundred-Year Mystery* was solved.

Suddenly a drum rolled and the audience became quiet. Hal walked to the front of the stage and said, "May I have the name of the fourth runner-up?"

A girl came onstage from the wings and handed him an envelope. He tore it open and announced, "The fourth runner-up is Helen Bramley!"

As the audience cheered, Mrs. Menken brought an arm bouquet and placed it in the girl's hands. Then she kissed and congratulated her.

The master of ceremonies now called for the name of the third runner-up. When he opened the envelope, he read the name Mary Weinstein. Again there was applause, flowers, and congratulations.

The second runner-up was Judy Irish. She was a great favorite with all the contestants, and received long, vigorous clapping from them as well as the audience.

Now there were only two contestants left— Amalie and Sally!

Mr. and Mrs. Benson were nervously holding hands and waiting breathlessly. Hal asked for the name of the first runner-up. He opened the envelope handed to him and read:

"The name of the first runner-up and the person who will take the place of the empress if she is not able to perform the duties assigned to her is— Amalie Sung!"

This meant that Sally Benson was the empress of the teen-age student talent competition! There was deafening applause as Mrs. Menken gave Amalie her bouquet, then picked up the gorgeous crown and placed it on the head of the winner!

"Sally Benson, our empress of the pageant!" she announced.

The orchestra began to play the special march that had been written for the occasion, and Hal sang it softly. The happy but tearful empress walked gracefully from the stage onto the runway. She marched in queenly fashion, smiling and bowing as she proceeded. When Sally spotted her parents, she threw a kiss to them, and this caused even greater applause.

Louise and Jean were alternately laughing and wiping tears from their eyes. They had never been happier in their lives! Sally finally returned to the stage and asked the orchestra to roll the drum again. It did so and the audience quieted down.

Sally took Hal's microphone and said, "Thank you all very much. A lot has happened since I arrived at Newport Beach. Sometime soon you will read all the details in the press. But for the moment I just want to tell you that I was kidnapped and might never have been here if it hadn't been for two wonderful friends, Louise and Jean Dana. Girls, please stand up so everyone can see who you are!"

The great pageant ended with a thunderous ovation for the teen-age detectives.

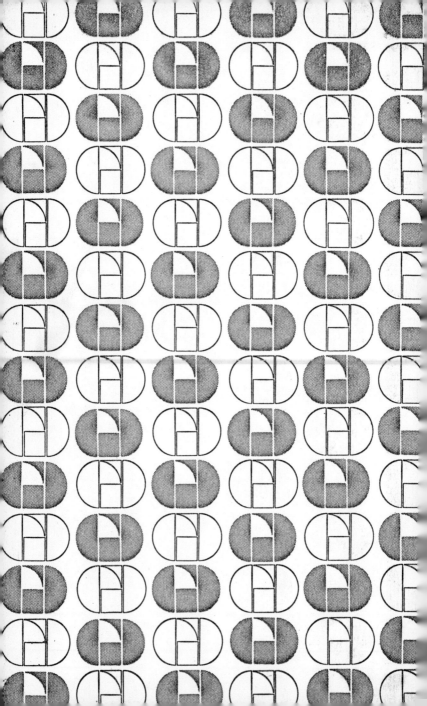